The Library of Congress has established a record for this title.
2009920624

ISBN 978-1-60743-027-8
I. My Eyes Are Green
Printed in the United States of America
Publisher
Datruth Publications
www.myspace.com/marcelemerson
Cover design: Leandre Fields
Layout: Datruth Publications

Dedication:

To: Vera Hollins and Tony Randolph Hunter

God, friendship, and family are what have gotten me through the rough times in my life. I miss you both and what a blessing you were in my life and so many others when you were alive. I will never forget you and I hope to join you in Heaven one day.

Maria:

Wishing you nothing but the very best Enjoy!

My Eyes Are Green

a novel

By: Marcel Emerson

Marcel Emerson

Maria:

Wishing you nothing but the very best Surgery!

[illegible]

PROLOGUE

Jennifer Peale

My mother and I both had the same green cat-like eyes, round button nose and long unruly auburn hair. She was the first of a long line of women that my father had married and later divorced. I remembered the day so vividly when I was introduced to the *first* woman who had said that she would be my second mother; but what she didn't know was that her days were numbered.

When I first heard Erykah Badu's CD and heard this verse on one of her tracks, "*My eyes are green because I eat a lot of vegetables, it don't have nothing to do with your new friend*", I felt sorry for the girl in the song. She had just gotten her heart broken, but she was trying to pretend it never happened in order to get over the pain. Denial to me meant death or despair and this song summed up my mother's life story. Living in denial was a pitiful way to live. I did my best to let things go that I had no control over, and move on.

When Daddy and his new wife came to pick me up for the first time I remembered feeling strange. I didn't understand why her and my father's arms were locked together like I had seen my mother and father do so many times. The look my mother had on her face as she watched with me was frightening. Her eyes were bloodshot red—you could tell that she had been crying—and she wore the coldest frown that I had ever seen on her face. I was too young at the time to understand that my parents were going through a divorce.

My mother was never the same after the visit from my father and his new wife. Before the visit, mother used to sing at church every Sunday faithfully. She belonged to three of the adult choirs, not belonging to the fourth because it was the Brotherhood Chorus. She also directed the youth choir where I first started singing. Growing up people used to tell me that my mother gave Whitney Houston a run for her money. The question was always, "Why did she ever stop singing and stop going to church?" She used to sing to me every night before she went to bed up until *that* visit. Sometimes at night I could still hear her soulful alto voice ringing throughout my ears. I longed for years to hear that voice again. I too wanted to become a singer just like my mother. I thought this would trigger something in her spirit to make her want to sing again

When I turned eighteen my mother committed suicide a week after I went to Spelman College in Atlanta, on a full voice scholarship. Nobody really knew why but I knew it was from a broken heart. Her death was so sudden, the next semester I changed my major to criminal justice, applied for financial aid, and set out to be a lawyer. I didn't ever want sing again.

Dontae Erickson

My eyes are green. Why? I don't know. My mother's eyes were brown – almost black. I never met my father. I must have gotten them from him. That, and my light skin. The only thing that my mother could tell me about my father was that he was a Jewish man who lived in North Carolina, and didn't want to have anything to do with her or me after I was born. That's the kind of relationship my mother and I had growing up. We would give each other "the brutal truth" no matter how much it hurt. She died of a heroin overdose when I was thirteen. After that, I moved from North Carolina to Seattle to live with my grandparents who were too old and could barely take care of themselves. They had been the only relatives at the time who were willing to take care of me.

I was sad and withdrawn when I first arrived in Seattle. Kids used to tease me because I was light-skinned. The whites used to say I was black and the blacks used to say that I was white. When I told them I was black they would tease me about having green eyes because most black children didn't have them. I was tall for my age. At thirteen, I was five-eleven almost six feet tall.

When I went to school for the first time in Seattle I had gym class with a kid who enjoyed playing basketball. He came right up to me and asked me if I played basketball too. I had never really given sports a try: I always just did my homework and looked after my little brother and my mom. So I answered his question by shaking my head – no. He was shocked at my response. I guess because I was even taller than he was, and he was the tallest guy in school before I had arrived. He introduced himself as Marcus Phillips, and then said he would show me some moves so I could make the school team.

Tryouts were in a week and we practiced at lunch and every day after school. I realized the first day on the court that I was a natural ball player. I was able to dunk the ball in the basket easily. I picked up on dribbling the ball and crossing it in between my legs when Marcus tried stealing it away from me. It only took me a week before I was able to beat him one-on-one, after he had beaten me in several games. I made the junior-high basketball team with ease, and he and I became instant best friends. Over the years, our friendship with one another grew closer as I adapted to my new life in Seattle.

In my junior year in high school I was able to participate in a program at the University of Washington. The program was geared towards minority students who were the first generation in their families to attend college. I spent the whole summer on campus taking college courses with other minorities in the Washington area.

I ate lunch at the Husky Union Building (HUB) alone everyday. I was the only one from my high school who attended the program and I didn't know anyone. I would however always run into this one particular guy eating alone—and always two tables from me. The two of us would glance at each other and occasionally speak, but never got around to introducing ourselves, until the last week of the, ten week, program. I guess since it was the last week, and we both were about to go our own separate ways he felt he had nothing to loose, so he asked me if I wanted to have lunch with him. I accepted his invitation and we sat together in the HUB for the first time. We started talking about what colleges we'd both hoped to attend one day and what we were going to major in once we got there.

After I got comfortable, out of nowhere he moved his head forward, close to mine, so I could be the only one who could hear him and he asked me if I ever had feelings for another guy. I was kind of shocked, but intrigued nonetheless. I didn't respond at first. He could see that I was getting red and I was beginning to become uncomfortable; (my cream-colored pale complexion always gave me away). I told him no, not at all. I then nervously stood up to excuse myself from the table.

"I will talk to you later," I said and just remembered after eating lunch together all this time we never exchanged names.

"Marcus," he blurted. "Your name is Dontae right? My name is Marcus," he said again.

I nodded my head, yes, and left in a hurry. I was nervous, but too scared to be interested, (these feelings I had: I was always made to feel ashamed of having them). When I got outside the HUB, my heart was racing, and I had a migraine headache, and I realized I had just lied. All I could think about since moving to Seattle were my feelings for Marcus, my best friend, and not the Marcus I had just left inside the HUB.

CHAPTER 1

Jennifer (J.P.)

O.K. it was like 8:45 am, Wednesday, August 7, 2003. I was extremely exhausted after driving twelve hours from Atlanta to Washington in my brand-new 2004 Land Cruiser. Daddy had hooked me up with this brand new truck as a graduation gift. The movers would have the rest of my belongings in Washington no later then Saturday. In May I'd graduated summa cum laude from Spelman College.

I woke up early enough to go get my truck cleaned, and pick up a few things for my new English basement apartment in the Shaw-Howard area of northwest. I still had enough time to buy something nice to wear to this club for happy hour. At five o'clock I was going with a sorority sister I hadn't seen in a while. It felt so good to be back on the east coast and out of the south. I felt like I was there way too long. The brothers there got on my last nerve, with their orange, yellow and lime-green outfits, thinking that they are "on top of the world." I dated three trifling brothers who bragged about being from the "dirty south." Boy, was I glad to give it all up. Now that I was in the nation's capital, I was going to make sure I stayed away from guys that talked with a twang, had a mouth full of gold teeth, or still sported Malcolm *X* processes or S-curls. I hated to be so shallow about my brothers, but a sister had to have her preferences. I was from "up-top" but Washington had to cut it for now. As long as I was out of Atlanta, it would do.

I had one more week left before I started my law school orientation at Georgetown University. Yale was my first choice but I didn't get in. But G.U. was a top ten school, plus it was in Chocolate City, so it would be an interesting three years for me. They said Washington had the finest black men, educated and employed. So this would be an experience, and I could most certainly work with those kinds of statistics.

I was glad that I decided to go directly to law school. Daddy tried to convince me to take a year off and do some traveling with him and his new wife. This was my father's fifth wife since I was seven years old! There should be a law against how many wives a man could have in his lifetime. This new woman was only three years older than me. I couldn't possibly see what a twenty-five-year-young woman would want with a fifty-two-year-old man, except for the obvious ... money. My father was just promoted to CEO of Eclectic Records, one of the elite companies in the record industry. He was a talent scout all his life, specializing in disco, funk and rhythm-and-blues singers and bands. That was how he met my mother—and all the rest of his wives. My mother, however, had no intention of becoming a professional singer.

My father saw my mother for the first time at a Gospel concert. She was a senior in high school at the time. She was the lead vocalist in a gospel girl-group performing at a New Year's Eve celebration for the upcoming 1979 year. My father was appointed through a connection of his as a talent scout for a new up-and-coming record label. He was responsible for going around the northeast region of the United States and bringing back talent to this small company in

Harlem trying to make a name for himself. My mother was seventeen at the time. She was a striking beauty standing 5'8, honey-brown complexion, auburn hair, and the greenest eyes he had ever seen on a black person in his life. But, what intrigued my father the most about my mother wasn't her eyes—it was her voice. Daddy once told me that my mother's voice was so crisp and clear, he thought she was lip-synching to a track at times. He knew when he'd met her that she *had* to come back to Harlem with him. He was prepared to sign her right on the spot. However, when he introduced himself he found out she wasn't yet eighteen. She was still seventeen and had six months of high school left; of course that didn't stop him from falling in love with her right then and there.

My mother was also an orphan and had lived in a convent all her life, raised by Roman Catholic nuns. She was a very simple girl. Her only aspirations were to become a nun, to imitate the strong dedicated ladies who raised her. She had "heard the calling" when she was thirteen years old. She once told me this when I was in the eighth grade. I saw a picture of one of these women once. It was in an old white ladies obituary that was sitting on the kitchen counter one day. My mother told me that this was one of the nuns who had raised her in the convent. She had just died of breast cancer. My mother was a wreck for a month after the old nun died.

My mother told me that the nuns at the convent wouldn't hear of her leaving school to become a rock singer. She said they could see, however, how much my mother was in love with my father. The nuns couldn't deny what they saw in my mother's eyes for my father every time she mentioned his name. They wanted the best for her, so they convinced her to stay in North Jersey and finish high school, and to take time to re-evaluate her decision to become a nun. For the next six months, my father came to visit my mother every weekend, making it impossible for her not fall in love. My mother graduated May 31, 1979, and the two were married June 5, 1979.

I was born in the spring on April 15, 1981. I was a happy child and the love that my parents had for each other radiated down to me. Imagine my utter confusion at seven years old, when I saw my dad holding another woman's arm. That experience shaped all my relationships with guys from that day forward. I loved daddy for always being there for me, but after what I saw in my mother's eyes when my father left, I realized I could never let a man have that much control over my life. Even today, I had a hard time trusting men. I guess that's why I have never had a serious boyfriend. When I was in high school, all the girls were envious of me, because most of the boys wanted my attention. My best friend and I would get into arguments because she would say that I was stuck up. I guess she thought so because I turned down every boy that asked me out on a date. What I realized now, after my mother committed suicide, was that growing up I was terrified of guys. I wasn't stuck-up nor did I think that I was better than anyone. I was raised in the church and taught to be God-fearing. I was also taught to believe that every human being was a child of God, and that we were all equal underneath His care.

Nonetheless, I too had my "diva days," when I believed my shit didn't stink. What could I say? I was blessed with a singing voice that could make an old lady weep, and above average looks that usually would get me into any club with VIP status in for free. I thanked God for that everyday, because life was hard for a girl if she was physically challenged, or if she was unable to accentuate her feminine pedigree.

In undergrad, to fit in with my sorority sisters, and deal with my fear of men, I learned to manipulate them. For me, they were just boy toys. My friend Kenya and I used to refer to men as "dem hoes" for our amusement. There were things most guys did for pretty girls like buy jewelry, concert and movie tickets, pay for hair, nail, and make-up maintenance. Many of my sorority sisters had men that would do these things for them and for a while, I looked to men to do the same for me. But this was only a phase I went through. Honestly daddy had already bought me everything that I had needed or wanted.

Since coming to Washington, I had to compete with more classy and sophisticated women that live in the area. I had bought several Vibe, Honey, and Black Hair magazines, all so I could give these girls a run for their money in style and pizzazz. I was in the south too long, and I couldn't step in the club tonight looking like I was a country bumpkin. J.P. was a northern fly girl, so I would be strutting my stuff to the nearest mall. I knew I needed to find I-395 south to take me to Pentagon City Mall, which was in Crystal City, less then ten minutes outside D.C. I had been to this mall when I visited D.C. before.

Kenya was picking me up from my apartment around five o'clock so we could get to the club in time for happy hour. I was really excited I was hanging with Kenya again. She graduated from Spelman a year before I did, and moved to D.C. to work as a personal assistant for a top-level executive in the FBI. She graduated cum laude with a degree in human resources. After graduation she went through a rigorous three months of training that all new employees were subject to at the "Bureau." She stayed with the FBI for three months after her training before quitting. She hated working for the government. She claimed it was boring with no excitement.

Now she was working as a staffing specialist for a national placement agency. She loved working at this new job. She said she felt great helping individuals find work. She did, however, complain about young African-Americans getting ripped off by these agencies. Most agencies billed companies more than double what they paid African-Americans.

She was working on her masters in human resources part-time at George Washington University for a year now. When she finished her program she planed to venture out on her own and start an agency similar to where she worked.

Kenya was my best friend back in Atlanta even before we both decided to pledge Delta. We were like sisters. I met Kenya because she was my resident advisor freshman year. At the floor meeting of the year she introduced herself to all the girls on my floor as Kenya Renee Bryant. She told us her major, what she planned to do when she graduated, and how Spelman in only one year had changed her life. She also told us that she was from Brooklyn, NY. Before she even mentioned where she was from, I knew she was from "up-top" so I was drawn to her familiarity instantly. And Kenya was a fly girl, so I knew I wanted to be her friend. Kenya was tall. She was about 5'7" with a smooth, immaculate ebony dark brown skin complexion. She had the lightest brown eyes I had ever seen on a person with her skin tone, and jet-black wavy hair that flowed to the middle of her back. She kind of reminded me of Maia Campbell, BeBe Moore Campbell's daughter, the actress who played on "In the House" with LL Cool J but slimmer and prettier. Kenya had an awesome shape. Back then, she was easily a size four or a five. If she was white, she probably would be a size zero, but she had the hips and booty like the rest of us black women. Her breasts weren't as big as she would have liked, but they were perky, and because she had a small waist line depending on what she was wearing it would give the illusion that they were much bigger than they were. When I first met her I just knew she had her pick of all the available and attractive men in Atlanta and I wanted to be right next to her picking and choosing. So I thought back then.

Throughout the whole meeting, all I could think about was, "this girl had mad flavor." Kenya was edgy and I could tell that she was from the streets. She held onto her edgy northern accent, and her "don't-fuck-with-me" N.Y. attitude. However, the Kenya I grew to love was sophisticated, smart and classy, despite growing up on the hardest streets of Brooklyn. One thing was certain; she didn't let the streets raise her. She took from the streets what would help her succeed in life, and when it was time for her to move on to something else, she moved on. The first year of knowing Kenya, I knew we were black women destined to be great friends. I never had another girlfriend, with whom I felt so comfortable, not even the girls I grew up with in Jersey. I could tell Kenya anything and not feel as though I would be judged or later have the information used against me. Most girls in high school were jealous of girls like me, but Kenya was just…, she was just different. She didn't tend to let other girls whether they were prettier or smarter intimidate her. She said I reminded her of her half-sister who died only a month after she moved to Atlanta.

Even though Kenya was great in so many ways on the outside, on the inside she suffered from a lot of demons. This was interesting to me since she had such striking beauty. She used to tell me that when she was growing up she hated what she looked like, and how she was a lot darker than her older sister. She was reminded of it every day.

The summer before my junior year Kenya and I had took a road trip to Alabama to see some of the new girls get inducted into our sorority at Alabama A&M University. We stopped by Wal-Mart to pick up gifts to hand out to the girls who were the same numbers as we were when we were on-line. When we got inside Wal-Mart we saw a full-figured older dark-skinned woman with two adorable little girls. The girls couldn't have been older than seven. Kenya and I stopped to exchange glances at the little girls. The girls were playing with each other, and had started getting rowdy and knocking merchandise off shelves. The woman wasn't paying any attention to the children at first.

Then out of nowhere, a Wal-Mart employee yelled, "Hey lady, are these your children? They are knocking things off shelves!"

The older dark-skinned woman looked around, obviously embarrassed, and screamed at the darker child, "I always have to tell your black ass to behave every time we go somewhere. Get your black nappy-headed ass over here and stand next to me." She yanked the little girls arm so hard I just knew she pulled it out of its socket.

The little girl started crying and said in a sad tone, "Butter was playing too, how come she never gets in trouble?"

"Your black ass always getting smart, don't talk back to me. When we get home, I am going to beat the devil out of you," the woman yelled. The other child just watched, expressionless. You could see in her eyes that this kind of yelling on her mother's part was not a rare occasion.

When Kenya and I got back to her car, she was in tears. I comforted her and that's when she explained to me how growing up she often went through something similar with her older sister. Kenya confessed of beatings she would get with extension cords for things that both her and her older sister would do together, and she had no memory of her older sister ever getting disciplined. Watching the woman at Wal-Mart treat that little girl so terribly brought back painful memories from her past.

Kenya and her older sister lived with their grandmother as children. Her mother used drugs during her childhood years and wasn't able to provide for two young girls. The two girls had different fathers; neither one had ever met them before. In the late seventies, their mother was a heroin addict. Kenya said that she was a prostitute and used the money to buy drugs. I had never been able understand how women could abandon their children just to get high. I didn't mean to be judgmental because everyone had a flaw or two… or three, but drugs just brought out the worst in people. Their grandmother, Ruby, was in her late thirties at the time when Kenya was born and sent to live with her. She held card parties in her basement which paid for their house in Brooklyn and provided food for them to eat and clothes for them to wear. Over the years, their mother would sober up about twice a year and would come to the house to braid their hair.

I was guessing that their Nana Ruby only pressed and curled their hair which made sense because my grandmother would always press mine. She said that their mother would also tell the girls how pretty and special they were. Kenya longed for the affection of her mother, and would pray that her mother would be sober sooner than later. Those visits were probably the only time that Kenya actually felt pretty and special and equal to her older sister. Kenya's mother when she was around didn't treat them differently like their Nana Ruby, who Kenya said was cruel and bitter. What was so ironic: Nana Ruby was dark-skinned as well, and was teased as a child growing up in the south. Instead of loving and embracing her granddaughter that resembled her to perfection, she resented and neglected her, and showered Kenya's sister Reba with praise, love and affection.

Despite all that, Kenya said that they adored one another. Reba was the oldest so Kenya looked up to her. Back when they were growing up, everything was given to Reba with no questions asked—you could say that she was spoiled rotten. Nana Ruby's card buddies would often see them playing in the yard or somewhere in the house and would comment on how pretty Reba was. "Your little grand baby is going to be a heart breaker one day," the men would say. "I wish my hair was as straight and fine as yours is," the women would confess to Reba. Never once did they mention or notice Kenya sitting or playing next to her sister Reba.

This story had brought back painful memories of my own mother withholding the love that I wanted so dearly to receive. I couldn't understand for the life of me how adults could be so cruel to children at times and not even know it. One thing I did know was that: this made my girl who she was, and she was a beautiful strong black woman in anyone's eyes today. I would always let her know that no one could take anything away from her.

Kenya and I had gone through a lot my first three years in Atlanta, with my mother committing suicide and me changing my major. So it was devastating to think that I would never talk to her again after my third year at Spelman. What made it even more sickening was I never thought a guy could interfere with the bond that we had between us. We both weren't considered to be the "relationship type" while we were in college. We both dated nonchalantly, we would joke with each other and would say, "we don't love dem hoes" whenever a guy would try to get serious on us, or swear that he was in love with either one of us. We'd say it was because they were whipped on the sex.

Back in college we weren't like those girls who thought it was their destiny for a tall, dark and strapping man to propose to us and take care of us for the rest of our lives. We never craved the attention of men the way most girls we hung out with did. It was always the other way around, until Kenya's senior year. One day, the Kappas at Morehouse, the all-men's school across the street, were throwing a party at a nearby club in Atlanta for their national convention they had in Atlanta that year. Cordel Roberts was a Kappa and he played for the Atlanta Falcons. As soon as we walked into the club he was sweating Kenya hard. She was initially ignoring his advances at first, because he wasn't really the type of guy that she was normally attracted to. Don't get me wrong, Cordel was fine, but "too pretty" was what Kenya would always say about guys that resembled Cordel. He stood about 6'4 and weighed around 225 pounds, absolutely carved of solid muscles. He had vanilla skin complexion and gray eyes. He wore his hair greasy, almost wet looking, kind of reminded me of Fabio or an Egyptian looking person. All the girls in Atlanta were crazy about him. He would often throw parties at his million-dollar mansion in the Stone Mountain area of Atlanta. There were rumors that only the really pretty girls with nice bodies were allowed to attend. They said a bouncer would be at the door checking body types and the faces of girls who they would allow to enter the mansion. I heard a lot of girls were denied entry because they either had jacked up teeth, their weaves looked a mess, or they were larger than a size 16, which they checked using a tailors' measuring tape. Kenya and I made it a point never to go out to one of the parties, because we felt it would be nothing but a bunch of groupies and men expecting cheap thrills from women because they had money to throw around. We'd heard that some of the girls at these parties got raped, and that guys tried to run trains on them—guys who'd get a kick out having sex with the same women at the same time. It was also said that most of the guys were very aggressive and wouldn't take no for an answer. So Kenya and I passed on every one of our invitations. We chose to go to clubs where the owners paid the bouncers to protect the well-being of the women who patronized their establishments. If a guy tried to step to her the wrong way, he'd quickly find a hard fist cracking his skull.

The whole night at the club Cordel kept our glasses filled with Moët, and Kenya still wouldn't accept his invitation to dance. So at about 2:00 a.m. after we had drunk three bottles of Moet, courtesy of Cordel, I encouraged her to accept his offer since it was getting late. "Girl, you might as well dance with him, he has been hooking us up all night with the champagne."

"J.P., I can't get over his hair, it almost looks better than mine," Kenya said patting her long wavy hair.

I had to laugh at that, "Now you know this is the south and these brothers can't help themselves. Just dance with him, you know he is fine as hell girl."

Kenya looked at her watch and said, "Well it is 2 o'clock now and if he keeps the Moet coming another forty-five minutes, it will be just in time for last call, and the DJ will have two more songs to play. I will dance with him for the last two songs. Those are usually the songs we have been waiting to hear all night anyway." Just like clockwork 2:45 came around and the DJ yelled on the loud speaker last call for alcohol and in a matter of seconds Cordel approached our table.

"Hey princess, the club is about to close. Come out onto the dance floor with me," Cordel sang and reached for Kenya's hand. Kenya grabbed his hand and let him help her out of her seat and onto the dance floor. When she got to the dance floor she turned her head back toward me and winked. The DJ started playing "Weak" by SWV, which was one of our favorite songs. In the middle of the song, as I was watching Kenya and Cordel dance, some guy came over to the table and asked me if I wanted to dance. I politely declined so I could finish watching my girl get her groove on with Cordel Roberts of the Atlanta Falcons. After the song was over Kenya walked over to the bar and Cordel followed her. I couldn't believe my eyes. My girl was writing her number down which broke a cardinal rule of clubbing; *never* give out your number in the club, always insist on taking his number and if you really like him call him a week later. When she finished writing her number down for him she placed it in the palm of his hand and whispered something in his ear, and they walked back to the table hand-in-hand. I couldn't believe it my girl was actually glowing at this point.

When they got back to the table, Cordel said to me, "Here is your friend back," kissed Kenya on the cheek and told her it was nice to finally meet her and dance with her and he was looking forward to talking to her tomorrow. We both watched his manly muscular silhouette walk out of the club with confidence and attitude like he had just won the super bowl.

By Christmas Cordel and Kenya were a steady couple. They spent most of their free time together when he was in Atlanta, or whenever Kenya could get away, Cordel would fly her to where he had a game. During the Christmas holiday, Kenya went to California to visit his family and fell in love with Cordel's mother and father. At this point, our “girl time” was dwindling down to late-night recaps of the week on Sundays before we went to bed and that was only if Cordel wasn't in town. We were no longer the dynamic duo; we were barely roommates. With her classes, work, and Cordel, we hardly had any time to hang out anymore. What was worse, once Valentine’s Day came around, Cordel proposed to her, she accepted of course and after that she practically lived with him. I still don't know why she didn't sublet her half of the apartment to someone and save the money.

After the engagement, Cordel bought her a brand new Lexus Coupe. The wedding was planned for June after she graduated from Spelman. I was happy for my girl, but sad that I was losing my best friend even though I knew she deserved someone special. I was her maid of honor at the wedding, and became the godmother of her children whenever she decided to have them, of course.

In the spring semester of my junior year, I started hanging with my sorority sister, Candice. Candice was from Philly and was also one of the fly girls on the campus. Candice, however, was wild; she drank too much, and she smoked weed almost everyday. She was the one who got me started smoking weed. She was 5'9, with mocha brown skin. She had dyed her hair reddish brown which complemented her brown complexion. She had a natural style about her and she had a really nice thin figure. She was very curvaceous even though she wore a size two. She modeled during the summer months in Europe, which was why she was such a party animal.

Over spring break, she had convinced me to go to Miami with her. She said she knew this basketball player for the Miami Heat that she went to high school with. We were going to stay with him. She called him her "play big brother." I thought that would be fun. I always wanted a close male friend, but that just never really worked out for me. I was game since I didn't have any plans. It was a little annoying having Kenya all in love and preparing for a wedding and graduation. I wouldn't have anyone to hang out with if I stayed in Atlanta for the week. I'd thought to myself, "What the hell," and went with Candice to Miami.

MIAMI WAS REALLY NICE and as soon as we pulled up to the beach house I knew I made the right decision to leave Atlanta and come to Miami for some much needed R&R. Candice's play brother, Kurt, turned out to be really nice and down-to-earth. Of course she didn't tell me he was gorgeous. I mentioned it to her while we were unpacking in his guest room. The room was phenomenal. It had a sliding double-paned glass door which was less than forty feet from the beach. It had its own bathroom with a Jacuzzi tub, and with marble counter tops and floors.

"Oh, Kurt, yeah he alright if you like that tall lanky basketball-player type, but you're not the only one, he has always had a lot of girls sweating him. I always thought it was because he played ball," Candice confessed to me. She also mentioned that he'd just broken up with her close friend Cherry who went to high school with them. They had two kids together but she stayed in Philly and they were never married. Cherry was Kurt's first and only love, but she'd broken his heart when she ended up getting pregnant by this hustler who she had a crush on her whole life, from around the way. He lived next door to her growing up but he would never give Cherry the time of day because he was four years older than her, and always looked at her as a little sister. Things all changed when Kurt started playing for the NBA and she was in the neighborhood flossing his money around. She started driving around in the hood in her new pimped out Cadillac. Buying out the bar whenever she went clubbing which was every weekend.

Candice said Cherry had always been fast and cheated on Kurt every time she had a chance, but this was the first time Kurt had distanced himself. Candice and Cherry used to be best friends, but they had a falling out in her freshman year in college because Cherry came to visit Spelman for Homecoming and ended up sleeping with Candice's boyfriend at the time. Candice didn't think she ever really loved Kurt. Cherry was one of those girls who expected men to treat her poorly and sought out guys who would use and disrespect her. Kurt was way too nice, he treated her like a queen and did everything she asked him to, no matter how stupid or ridiculous the request was. Like the time Cherry told Kurt she needed seed money so she could open up a barbershop in her neighborhood, and the chile didn't have a cosmetology license or even knew how to cut hair. But of course Kurt gave her the ten thousand dollars.

Kurt had been in several fights and had even gone to jail fighting other dudes that she would cheat with. The only reason she stayed with him so long was because she knew he was going to the NBA. Candice never got in their personal business, but she was glad that he'd finally found out on his own what type of person he was dealing with. It was just sad that they had two kids together.

THE FIRST COUPLE DAYS IN MIAMI all we did was lay out on the beach, smoked weed and drank Margaritas. "This was the life," I thought. In the middle of the week we'd went to one of Kurt's basketball games. Candice and I sat up in one of the skyboxes owned by one of Kurt's endorsers and sipped champagne and watched the New Jersey Nets, my team, whip up on Miami. I tried not to get too excited since I was in Miami and a guest of one of Miami's players.

After the game, we went to an after-party for one of Kurt's teammates. He was celebrating his 25th birthday at a local "hot spot" in Miami. There were so many celebrities at the party, I felt like I didn't fit in. Candice was acting as if this was how she always partied. She was already tipsy from all the champagne she drank at the game. At the club she'd met a guy who kept buying us glasses of Cristal. I'd had enough after two glasses, but she kept drinking and drinking. I would have been on the floor after so many drinks. Just when I thought that I'd seen enough, Candice stumbled onto the dance floor with her new friend that was buying the bottles. I watched her back-it-up and rub her booty all over his crotch until I couldn't take anymore and walked back to the VIP section to see what Kurt and his friends were up to.

The VIP section had three purple crush velvet sofas in a triangle in the middle of the room, with enough space in between each couch to sit down, and a gold centerpiece where glasses of alcohol and empty Moet and Cristal bottles in chillers were placed. There were four large plasma TV screens, one on each wall of the room, a full bar towards the back, and along each wall there was a small circular table and two chairs that were five feet tall.

I saw Kurt sitting at one of the tables alone. He was drinking a beer and watching the recap of the game that was on one of the plasmas. The room reeked of Marijuana and a combination of expensive perfumes, giving it a truly psychedelic atmosphere. The only thing missing was mushrooms. I didn't feel like staying and getting used to the smell, so I walked out to go to the bathroom. Before I could get there one of Kurt's teammates tapped me on my shoulder.

"Hey you're Jennifer right?" He said.

"Yeah, but call me J.P., everyone does" I said, checking out his merchandise. I didn't notice any ring, so he passed the pre-qualification criterion.

"Oh, okay J.P., it is really nice to finally meet you. I have been checking you out since you and Candice walked into the club. Since she is on the dance floor, I thought this would be a perfect time to introduce myself, and see why a pretty woman like you is hanging around a guy like Kurt," He teased. "By the way, my name is Daniel, but everyone calls me Dee for short." He wasn't bad-looking at all, and he was smooth. At this point I was a bit more interested, so I decided in my mind to play along and see where this would go. Didn't matter anyway because Candice was off doing her thing and had left me to fend for myself.

What I noticed about Dee was that he stood out from most of his teammates. He seemed like he was on a different plane. For one, he was the only one who had on slacks and a nice shirt and loafers. He smelled good too. It was like he put on just enough cologne to make you want to get closer, and smell him again to figure out what actual scent he was wearing. Most of the players, including Kurt, came to the club with basketball jerseys or throw-back shirts with jeans or shorts. Most of them were sporting the latest Jordans or name-brand tennis shoes. I liked the fact that he cared about his appearance which made me want to know more about what kind of person he was. Turned out he was twenty-eight and he graduated from Syracuse with a degree in psychology.

After I used the restroom, Dee and I sat at a booth near the dance floor so that I could keep an eye on Candice's drunken ass. I didn't realize how long we were talking until the DJ came on the speaker to announce last call. I was so annoyed, because by this time Candice was nowhere in sight. I took this as my cue to end the conversation with Dee to go look for my friend. He offered to help me look for Candice, but I declined, telling him that I could manage fine on my own. I figured that she was probably just at the bar getting another drink before it closed. He said that he would wait for me at the booth until I found her, which I thought was nice of him.

I looked all over the club for Candice, but she was nowhere to be found. I went to check the VIP room so that I could catch a ride back to the house with Kurt, and he also was nowhere to be found. I started to get really upset. I couldn't believe that drunk bitch left me at the club, for some wack-ass brother, I thought. I called her cell phone three times but got no answer. When I dialed Kurt's house number, the maid, Maria, picked up on the first ring and said that Candice hadn't came back to the house. She said that Kurt was upstairs making love to his pillow, knocked out. She told me to catch a taxi to the house and she would be there to open the door for me. As I was putting my phone back in my purse, Dee came closer to me and said the club was about to close and asked me if I was okay. I explained to him that Candice must have already left with the guy she was dancing with and that Kurt was at the house already. I was trying not to let Dee know how irritated I was, but it was obvious. I couldn't believe that Candice would get so drunk and leave me at a club in Miami where I have never been before. I ended up accepting a ride from Dee because he seemed level-headed, and he insisted on taking me home instead of allowing me to catch a cab.

Thank goodness he didn't try anything as he was driving. I couldn't take another night's surprise. As soon as we pulled up to Kurt's house, Dee asked me if he could take me out before we left to go back to school. Considering that he was such a gentleman, I told him that most likely we would be able to get together before we left to go back to Atlanta. I was still somewhat unsure, so I left it open by saying that we would play it by ear. Also, I didn't know what Kurt and Candice had planned. It was already Thursday and we had planned to drive back on Sunday morning. I could tell he was used to getting what he wanted by most girls, because he seemed shocked that I hadn't agreed right away. He was trying to get me to commit to seeing him the next night for dinner, but I didn't budge. Giving him the notion that I had enough pressuring, I reached over and gave him a hug and a kiss on his cheek. Thanked him for the ride and stepped out of his truck. When I had got up to the front door I turned back around and I caught him staring at my butt. He didn't even look up and notice that I had turned my head back around. Men were so trivial. I turned all the way back around, winked back at him and he pulled off.

I HAD WOKEN UP THE NEXT morning to Candice coming out of the bathroom, wrapped in a towel. She had just finished taking a shower in the guest bathroom. Before I could even say good morning, she immediately started apologizing about the previous night of leaving me at the club with no ride or arrangement to get home. She said she could barely remember going to the club and all she could really remember was waking up at a strange man's house that she didn't know butt-ass naked. She said that he was standing over her telling her he needed to take her home because he had to go to work.

I got on her case about drinking so much and how dangerous it was to leave a club with a guy that she had just met. She knew that what she did was irresponsible and reckless. I began feeling sorry for her because I kind of figured that this was not an isolated incident. I remembered hearing another sorority sister comment on something similar she did when they were in Cancun last Memorial Day. Candice started making excuses about this incident. I listened to her ramble on about how she wasn't that drunk and how she never met crazy guys and how she was alright. I didn't say anything else. What could I have said? If she loss control like that often, there is no telling what went on when she was with strangers, or whether or not condoms were being used.

I left her crazy ass sitting right there, and I jumped in the shower. Some things are better left unsaid. My silence said plenty; plus, I wanted to go to the gym and continue my weekend and not have to deal with this.

After the gym, Candice and I had a late breakfast at a restaurant on the boardwalk of South Beach. We sat outside and watched the beautiful people of South Beach rollerblade and jog along the boardwalk. Spring Break attracted a lot of college students from around the country. People came just to enjoy the sunshine and get away from all the books and hours of studying for just a week. I would like to personally thank whoever invented spring break because I knew they were thinking about me. Again, I commended myself for making the decision to get away from Atlanta, even if it was just for a week. I only wished that Kenya was down here enjoying this sunshine with me. I knew, though, that she and Cordel were busy in California planning for their wedding.

When Candice and I got back to the house, Kurt announced that he was going to throw a going away party for us at his beach house Saturday night. He mentioned that he'd already invited half of Miami. I was floored when I heard the news, but Candice quickly spoiled my mood by stating that Kurt just needed a reason to show off his new home to the people of Miami. I didn't care either way. I was already thinking about what I was going to wear.

THE DAY OF OUR "GOING AWAY" party was spectacular! The sun was shining brightly in the sky; the air was warm, there was a faint breeze hugging my skin. I thought about wearing my denim cat suit. I didn't want to look too raunchy, but I really didn't have any other place to wear it. Kenya and I both saw the outfit when we were in New York for Thanksgiving shopping in the Village. We had to toss a coin on who was actually going to be able to purchase it. I knew I saw it before her, but she claimed she saw it before me. Our rule when we go shopping was whoever saw something first would get first dibs, but in this case since we saw it at the same time we had to flip a coin, and luckily tails never fails. After thinking about how I won the scramble and toss up, I decided to wear it. I must say I looked mighty good in the jumper.

After getting dressed, Candice and I decided we would do a grand entrance once the crowd got thick. We didn't want the guests to come in and check us out, we wanted to make an appearance and check everyone else out. Kurt said folks would be arriving around ten p.m., so we had thought a little after midnight would be a great time for us to stroll into the party.

In order to help us get things together for the party and loosen up a bit of our inhibitions, Kurt had brought us a bottle of Don P to the room. Of course ole' "alcoholic veteran" was ever-so-excited to have a bottle for us brought to the room while we got ready. We turned on the radio to Miami's current hip-hop station and had a party of our own listening to the latest jams while sipping champagne, applying make up, and styling our hair. It was quite fun and we took our time doing so.

I decided to have Candice cornrow the front half of my hair, and had the back of it pulled back and the ends curled. I saw Monica, the singer, rock this hair style once at a club in Atlanta, and I knew Candice was a good braider so she hooked me up. Even though I liked what I was wearing, I was torn between the denim cat suit and a salmon colored summer dress that tapered around the waist. It had thin spaghetti straps that showed my shoulders and back. I decided to keep on what I was wearing because Candice reminded me of how the summer dress made me look like I was going to a cookout or bridal shower and not a hot baller's party in Miami.

Candice decided to wear a black one-piece too-tight number. She had to keep pulling her dress over her breasts to keep them from being exposed. I teased her and said she is destined for a wardrobe malfunction if she didn't change before she hits the party, but to no avail; she had already made up her mind. What set her look off was her hair. It was wild, teased and crazy all over her head, with a black rayon scarf tied around the hairline of her head. Big hair was sexy and sent the message that I knew she wanted to send: "I am available and unrestricted."

Midnight had finally arrived and we walked out to the party to hear Notorious B.I.G.'s "One More Chance" playing. I noticed a group of people standing by the bar waiting on cocktails to be served. Candice and I decided to walk out to the deck adjacent to the great room to get some fresh air and to view the beautiful beach. There were several people out on the deck sitting on the cranberry-colored cushion patio furniture. Kurt must have had about twenty different pieces of chairs, sofas, stools, love seats, and he had palm trees in planters situated around the deck, giving it a resort-type feel. Also, there was a bar at the far right end of the deck where women with fake boobs were serving drinks. We'd made our way over to the bar since the one inside seemed more packed than this one was. I ordered another glass of Don P and Candice ordered a Long Island iced tea. I didn't want booze that night so I stuck to the champagne. We decided to walk down to the beach to see what was going on down there. Kurt had installed a tent on the beach with a hardwood dance floor that was removable and there was a DJ spinning on the turntable. We could see from the deck that most of the crowd was down by the beach because the night was perfect and the air was warm, with a cool breeze coming from the ocean.

When we had got close to the tent, I recognized the popular rap group out of Miami, 2 Live Crew. Trina, the rapper, was with them and they were talking. I was surprised by how pretty she was in person. Her videos didn't do her any justice. She did look a little shorter than I anticipated. Candice said she had met 2 Live Crew a couple of times before. They weren't as rowdy as their music portrayed them.

When we got to the dance floor we danced for a couple of songs together, then Candice ran into someone she knew and she left me on the dance floor alone. I couldn't believe she set me up again. My mistake this time—to think that Candice would want to hang out with me during the party. I tried not to feel embarrassed because I didn't know anyone, so I drank my champagne and two-stepped off the dance floor to the beat. I decided to walk back up to the deck and get another glass of champagne and hopefully meet back up with Candice later.

As I was approaching the deck, I had to do a double-take because I saw Cordel, Kenya's fiancé, holding a girl that looked like a model by the waist. The woman was a six footer, and with the pumps she was wearing that easily took her to 6 ft 5'. After taking my eyes off the Glamazon of a women she was, I remembered that he was supposed to be in California with Kenya and his parents planning their wedding over the break. He looked shocked to see me and apparently he figured that I wasn't happy to see him all up in that woman's face. Cordel immediately dropped his hands from the young woman's waist as he focused in on my facial (I-am-going-to-tell-Kenya) expression. He whispered something in her ear and walked towards me. Despite the fact that I was mad as hell for being left alone again by Candice. I was also cold because the breeze was getting on my nerves, messing up my hair. But, I was still able to sense that he had been drinking a lot because he was swaying from side to side and his eyes looked glossy.

"Hello J.P.," he murmured, "It's good to see you out of your element." Cordel was not looking at my face but his eyes were directed towards my breasts in a sly sort of way that immediately pissed me off. What the hell? Was his ass sizing his best friend's girl up and down, like he wanted to holler or something? This was it for me.

"Cordel, I came down here with Candice for Spring Break, she went to high school with Kurt. Aren't you supposed to be planning a wedding or something?" I snapped.

"Oh yeah, Kenya and my moms got all that under control. I had to leave a couple of days early because I was meeting with the owners of the Miami Dolphins. They're thinking about recruiting me to come play down here. Kurt and I have the same agent, and I always chill with him when we're in the same city. This is a small fucking world." He got all that out in less than one minute. Kenya mentioned before how he shoots off out the mouth when he was lying.

Playing along, I said, "Tell me about it. So who is that model you were all up on?" I rolled my eyes to let him know that I disregarded his alibi.

"Who? Keisha? That is my play lil sister," Cordel replied.

"Well, you must be into incest, because you sure were holding her close." I said. I knew he was lying because I had never heard of no damn Keisha from Kenya. This type of shit was exactly why it was so hard to trust men, especially ones with a lot of money, and with big egos. They were never satisfied. For a quick second, I wondered if there were any men out there that truly believed in monogamy or was it just the women born with that stupid one–man-one-woman philosophical trait? Why couldn't we have more fun and sleep at night without the guilt of feeling loose? What a double standard.

I snapped out of it and smacked my lips, "MMMMH"! Well, let me go find Candice. Be sure to tell Kenya I said 'hi'." I tried ending the conversation and walking away but he grabbed me with an aggressive force and turned me back around.

"Hold up girl, why it got to be all like that? I am just trying to enjoy myself while I am in Miami. Why don't you help me? Let's chill?"

"Boy, paleaze!" I thought about how we used to say that on the playground when the pissy boy wanted to get too close. "You better get on the next flight to go meet up with Kenya, since you two are getting married, that was if you're still getting married."

"See that is what I'm talking about, women always jumping to conclusions. I am just having a couple of drinks and enjoying the Miami weather. No harm in that. It's not my fault that a brother is irresistible and ladies cannot get enough of me."

"Yeah, ok Cordel. But as I was saying, I gotta go find Candice so I can start enjoying myself as well. Enjoy the scenery."

Just when I thought that he couldn't cross any other lines, he said, "J.P., you sure are looking good in that cat suit. Looks like you've been filling out these days. Is that southern food finally kicking in?"

"Now you know you just crossed the line. What the hell would Kenya think if she knew you were checking me out, on top of just groping your play lil sister?" I was angry and I didn't want to have a loud confrontation over this nonsense, so I was hoping that he would just back off and let me walkway. As I turned to walk away again, he grabbed me around my waist tight and pulled me towards him. My body slapped up against his within half a second, and I hit my head on his chest. Considering the champagne I had been drinking all night and all that was happening, I felt a migraine coming on. On top of that, Cordel was really tripping and I was getting even more delirious. "Cordel let me go; this shit is not cool. I have been drinking and you are about to make me throw up all over your new Jordans," I lied.

He finally released me after palming my ass. I couldn't believe that Cordel was such a jerk. I quickly walked back to the dance floor on the beach not looking back to where I just left Cordel. I wanted to leave this party but since I was staying here I thought I had better find Candice and try to enjoy what I could of my last night in Miami. We planned to get on the road and head back to Atlanta no later then 10:00 a.m. the next day.

When I'd finally caught a glance of Candice, she was walking along the beach bare foot with the guy that she was dancing with earlier. I had no idea that she was going to spend all her time with this guy, but whatever. When Kenya and I used to go out, we would never be away from each other for that long, and even if we danced with someone else, there was like a two - song maximum before we would regroup in the ladies room for some gossip. This chick was all about a man. I'd made a note to myself to get some new friends once I got back to Atlanta because Candice didn't make the cut in the hanging-out-with-me department.

I didn't feel like walking back up to the house for fear that I might run into Cordel so I just went to the bar under the tent and got another drink. As I was walking away from the bar, Dee, Kurt's teammate, brushed up against me on purpose and said hello. Even though Dee was cute, he wasn't really my type of guy. There was just something different about him that I didn't really vibe with. However, I was so happy to see a familiar face after my altercation with Cordel and being ditched by Candice that I gave him all my attention at the moment just to pass the time.

We talked for about an hour and walked along the beach away from everyone, but just close enough to hear the music from the party slightly. While we talked, he left me twice to go get us refills on our libations. Both times when he left I just stared at the water and the rocks watching Mother Nature and all her glory. I came to find out he was born and raised in Holland. He had gotten a college scholarship to play at Syracuse, and he was pretty intelligent. After he graduated, he played two years in Europe before he decided to try out for the Heat, and he had been playing for them for four seasons. He told me that his family was originally from the island of Aruba. He also said that both his parents were from there and mixed with Dutch, which explained his light complexion and the reason why I'd felt he was different from most black men that I knew. He seemed to be a really down-to-earth guy, and I was sure he would make a real nice boyfriend and husband for someone, just not me. I needed someone who was born in America who I could identify with more culturally.

After we talked, Dee was going home to pack. He said that now that the season was over, he was going back to Holland to visit his family because his youngest sister was getting married.

We ended our conversation. I was a little buzzed and tired. I didn't see Candice anywhere so I decided to call it a night and head back to the room and get my things together so that we could leave the next day. When I got back to the room everything was in the place as we left it. The flat iron was still plugged in next to the large mirror above the dresser, and my summer dress was thrown against the chair. I went to the closet to retrieve my suitcase so I could start packing and as I was bending down I heard the door crack open. I jumped when I heard the noise and turned around to see Cordel enter the room quietly and lock the door behind him.

I was startled by his entry into the room that I just froze in place. It all seemed to happen so fast that I did not even have time to think about what he could possibly want. I wondered if he had followed me back to the room. He was nowhere in sight when I entered the house and I figured he left. He immediately walked over to where I was and pulled me up. I was still bending down in the closet as he pulled me closer. I could smell the strong odor of liquor on his breath. I really couldn't believe what was happening to me. I struggled to be released from his grip but Cordel was much too strong for me. However, I couldn't stop trying to free myself impulsively and with every struggle to break free, his fingers pierced deeper into my flesh. I could feel the pain and see my arms turning purple from his tight grip. I kept screaming, "Get the hell off me," but I knew nobody could hear us because of the music. This still did not stop me from trying to get away. Cordel then turned me around with my back on his chest and my backside pressed up against is erect penis. I could feel the bulge coming through his jeans as soon as he turned me around. He then moved one hand down to my panties and held me close against him with his other hand, still making it impossible for me to get away. As soon as his fingers slid into my vagina, I began crying and stopped struggling. I couldn't believe what was going on. He then took his fingers from inside of me and I heard him unzip his pants just as he was about to enter me raw. By this time my screams turned into sobbing tears and streams of salty water petals ran down my face. I could hear my tears hit the floor. I thought to myself about other women who were raped every day and was so upset with myself for not being more safe and cautious. How could this happen to me? Why, God? Just then, I heard beating at the door. Cordel let me go abruptly and I fell to the floor real hard and busted my lip. My face was wet and my hair hung like a damp mop from all the sweating I had been doing. When I hit the floor, I hit my nose as well. Blood was everywhere and my bottom lip was throbbing.

I heard someone kick open the door. I was afraid to look up but I heard Kurt screaming, "What the fuck is going on in here?" For a moment I felt guilty as if I had done something wrong. A few seconds later Kurt picked me up off the floor and asked me if I'd needed an ambulance. I was too humiliated and embarrassed about the whole situation. All I could do was cry and tell him to go get Candice. I didn't want anyone to see me in the state that I was in. All I wanted to do was go back to Atlanta and act like it never happened. Cordel left the room and the house as soon as Kurt forced his way into the guest room.

When Candice finally got to the room and was debriefed by Kurt on what had just transpired between Cordel and me, she began crying, telling me that I needed to call and press charges. There was no way I could call the cops. The whole world knowing that I had been violated by an idiot was too much attention for me. Also, I knew that I would be an easy target for the media and many of his fans would've portrayed me as some kind of groupie. I had my whole life to live and I couldn't live in the shadows of a humiliating public scandal. So I decided to take a scalding hot bath in the tub. When I got out the tub, Kurt told me he cleared out the party. He'd brought me gauzes for my nose and my lip and Ibuprofen to ease the pain so I could get some sleep.

Candice and I fell asleep next to one another, holding each other for dear life. The next morning, Kurt said that he'd made reservations for the both of us to fly back to Atlanta first class and that he would have Candice's' car shipped to her first thing Monday morning. He kept apologizing to me for what happened and told me he understood why I didn't want to press charges. He said that he had seen this sort of behavior many times before, but this was the first and last time it would ever happen in his home. I reassured Kurt that it wasn't his fault, that he had no ideal that Cordel would do something like he did. Another part of me was afraid to go back to Atlanta, because I knew I had to inform Kenya of what her fiancé had done to me. Considering how sneaky he was, I figured that he might try to beat me to the punch. Even though I knew Kenya so well, I had no clue how she would react. I was so confused, angry and disgusted at the same time. Also, I was hurt by the mere fact that Cordel would intentionally hurt my best friend by hurting me physically and mentally.

When we got back to Atlanta, there was no time to think about what happened in Miami. I knew I needed to talk with Kenya but my classes and spring rush for my sorority took up all of my time which was good. I didn't see too much of Candice when we got back either. She was a theater major so we had no classes together and I wasn't in the mood for clubbing and partying. Her personality was perfect for theater: unpredictable and unstable, just full of drama.

THREE WEEKS AFTER SPRING BREAK on a Thursday night, Kenya came to the apartment unexpectedly. She startled me when I heard someone trying to open the door, so I opened it and saw her standing there. I had been at the dining room table studying for a statistics class that I had been trying to avoid since coming to college. Math wasn't particularly my best subject and it always required me to spend extra hours studying and several hours seeking help during the professor's office hours.

I could tell something was up with Kenya when I saw her. Ever since she had been dating Cordel, she had been very upbeat, almost as if she was glowing. This time, however, she looked as though she hadn't slept in days, and a dark cloud was hovering above her head. I said before she could even get all the way in the apartment, "We need to talk."

"Yes, I know," Kenya responded and took a seat across from me at the table. "So Cordel says that he saw you in Miami over spring break at a party, and you threw yourself on him, trying to get him to cheat on me and ruin our relationship." Kenya was staring directly at me with tears coming from her face. She almost couldn't get the word relationship out her mouth. She said it in such a whisper I could barely make it out. I could tell she was looking at me to see if what I was going to say was the truth. All I felt was guilt because I had waited so long to tell her what really happened, but I didn't know how to. I lacked courage.

Tears started rolling down my face, as I began to speak. I wasn't caught off guard because I thought that Cordel would twist the story around on me and make me look like the bad one. I was just unprepared to tell Kenya my side because I thought that she might blame me for some reason. I didn't know why I felt that way, but I did.

"Kenya, this is really hard for me because I have been avoiding you since I got back. I didn't know how to tell you. I didn't try and sleep with Cordel. You have to know I would never do something like that to you. I love you like you were my sister. Since I have been in Atlanta, we have always been there for each other. The last thing that I would want to do to you is hurt you, which is why I couldn't bring myself to tell you that Cordel raped me in Miami."

"He did what!?" Kenya screamed. "You have got to be joking! We are planning to get married in less then two months!" She was fuming at this point. I stood up to walk over to where she was sitting and hug her, but by the time I got over to where she was she grabbed her keys from the table, jumped up from her seat and darted out the apartment door.

That was the last time I had spoken to Kenya before I'd gotten back in touch with her to tell her I was moving to Washington. She graduated from Spelman that May, moved to D.C. and never married Cordel. I tried reaching out to her several times that semester; she never returned any of my phone calls. I did see her at graduation, but she was too far away from me to say congratulations and when I went to look for her she was gone.

However, a week before moving to D.C. something had told me I needed to get back in touch with her. We were way too close not to stay friends, and I hoped that she would know that I would never in my life do anything deliberately to hurt her. I'd gotten Kenya's number from another sorority sister who lived in D.C. as well. I was so delighted to find out that Kenya was no longer mad at me; actually she confessed that she was never mad at me.

Kenya had known what type of person Cordel was when he proposed to her; she was just too caught up and excited that someone as successful and good-looking would want to be with her for the rest of his life. Plus, he bought her a Lexus, and paid off all of her student loans. Kenya didn't want to think about having to struggle again. She confided in me that Cordel was very abusive and that he had several women calling the house. She even walked in on him with one of his teammates having sex with one of the freshman girls at Spelman.

But after the incident that he'd pulled with me, she said she had to leave him. She said at first he thought she was joking, and that she would come crying back. But when Kenya moved to D.C. Cordel knew she wasn't playing. He tried threatening to murder her if she didn't marry him. It was so bad that she had to get a restraining order against him.

The last thing she told me was that she felt guilty about how things went down, and how she wasn't there for me in my time of need. I let her know that there were no hard feelings, and that I appreciated her honesty even if it took some time. She said she couldn't wait to get reacquainted with me again, and she assured me that I would love D.C., and that she would show me the ropes just like she had when I moved to Atlanta. And the first showing was Republic Gardens for happy hour.

CHAPTER 2

Dontae

I had dreamed about going to law school ever since I was seven when my mother and I used to watch the Cosby Show every Thursday. My mother resembled Phylicia Rashad. She had Phylicia's long shapely legs, perfect vanilla brown skin tone with picture-perfect cheekbones, and long black hair. I would dream at night that I was one of the Huxtable kids and my mother was Clair Huxtable, a lawyer with a strong feminine personality, dignified and classy. My mother resembled her, but her personality was quite the contrary. She had no self-confidence; she let people abuse her and treat her like she wasn't a human being. I despised my mother when I was younger and at times I tried my best to be nothing like her.

However, as I got older, I realized that I was more like my mother than I would like to admit. When I was younger I longed to be a lawyer; I enjoyed watching Clair Huxtable because it became like a dream, more like a fairy tale that I could watch and only hope for during that time in my life. The Cosby show was an enjoyment and became my motivation while I was younger and Clair Huxtable represented a person I missed in my life, someone I wished was my real mother.

I used to lie a lot and get into fights in school because I was such a troubled child. I wanted my mother to be a better person; I thought that if she were a better person, then I would feel better about myself. That is when I first started hating the person I was, and wouldn't allow myself to become anything like my mother. Growing up I became the center of lies, and self-hatred, not wanting to be myself, not really understanding that being me was okay, and being what I thought other people wanted me to be wasn't ok. This was a struggle for me today, something that I had to deal with every day, trying not to be what others wanted me to be, and accepting myself for who I was and what God made me.

I wanted my mother to be a strong person. This meant she picked the right man and if she made the wrong choice in choosing a man, she had enough self-esteem not to let the heartache and pain drag her spirit down; where it affected her life and the people around her – especially her kids. I wanted her to choose a man that would help her take care of her family. A man that helped her build a successful and comfortable life, or she developed the strength to do it alone if necessary. But unfortunately that never happened.

Even though Clair Huxtable got me interested in law as a child that was not the reason I wanted to be a lawyer today. I had grown up a lot since I was first introduced to the Cosby show. I no longer despised my mother, but there were a lot of things that I didn't understand about her that frustrated me, even today. My ambition to become a lawyer was something that had given me strength and determination at times when I doubted myself and wanted to give up. The dream kept me focused when I felt like I was alone and discouraged. It was not just the title lawyer that gave me the strength, it was more the accomplishment of knowing that I came from very humble beginnings and I worked hard in becoming successful for no one other than myself. I wanted a rags-to-riches story for myself, so I could someday help other children that grew up like me. Let them know that there was another way. So what, your mom wasn't there for you. So what you barely knew your daddy.

Empowering the disadvantaged was going to be a part of my existence. (Everyone had to do what was necessary to ensure their own happiness. Never look for anybody to treat you better than you were willing to treat yourself except for God.) But in my twenty-one years of life, I had seen many folks treat themselves poorly. I'd made a vow to myself that I would never put anyone before me and do what was best for me at all times. This may sound selfish, but when you looked back at your life and you realized that nobody had your best interest at heart, you would understand where I was coming from. Don't get me wrong, there had been positive people in my life that I looked up to; that touched my life in many ways. But none of them were devoted to just me, like a mother or father would be to their children. So growing up without your parents' devotion makes you more independent, self-centered and yes selfish to a certain extent.

Now that I was in D.C. for the first time, I was shocked when I got to the airport and saw so many black people, people who looked like me, in one place. I was staying with my friend Felicia, who I went to high school with. She was now living in Washington, and her roommate was supposed to pick me up from the airport, because Felicia was at her job's annual crab feast. The only description I had was that she was a short thin brown-skinned girl. As I walked down the escalator to the baggage claim area all I saw were brown-skinned women. I only planned on staying with Felicia and her roommate until I found my own place hopefully before law school started. I sure didn't plan on sleeping on their couch for too long.

I heard so many different things about the east coast growing up, and I was really excited to be here. Most people thought I was crazy moving so far for law school, but things that most people would miss are things I was trying to escape.

I did have family that would miss me and I would miss them too, but I needed a significant change in my life. While I had acquaintances and friends back home in Seattle, nothing was so great that I would miss the opportunity to go to Georgetown Law School. Harvard was my first choice, but I was waitlisted and by the time they finally sent the letter and said that they wanted me to come I had already fallen in love with Georgetown. The thought of being in the nation's capital, and living in Chocolate City excited me.

While in undergrad when I first started using the Internet, I would always log into gay black male chat rooms, and all the boys that I would meet were either from D.C., Atlanta or New York. Of course you would find your "Lone Rangers" like me, out in no-black-man's-land, like Denver, Milwaukee or Salt Lake City. But like I said most of the boys and especially the boys with the nice bodies and the best stories to tell about sexual escapades, parties and clubs were concentrated in D.C., Atlanta, and New York City. So I knew I wanted to be in one of those metropolitan cities sometime in my life.

When most people thought of Seattle, they thought that there were no black folks who lived there. I didn't know where people got that idea from, because there was a large black population in Seattle neighborhoods and high schools. In fact, Mayor Norm Rice was a black man and had been the mayor of Seattle for as long as I could remember. Don't get me wrong, Seattle was no D.C., but it definitely wasn't Vermont or Iceland either.

I always felt like I didn't belong in Seattle; I felt like a captive in prison, waiting for my sentence to end. I wanted to explore the world, and do the things that I had always dreamed of. I had so many things that I felt I needed to do and couldn't because the city wasn't the platform for it. I couldn't be myself and I definitely couldn't express myself, because I felt that my family and the people I grew up with wouldn't accept me for the person I was. I have always been different; even when I was thirteen I was wise beyond my years. I wasn't like any of the other kids I went to school with or lived in my neighborhood. I spent a lot of time by myself, watching television. Most kids my age admired positive people and had adult role models surrounding them. Or at least I thought that was the case. But I always felt I was different from the other boys I grew up with. So I isolated myself for the most part, because I was afraid to truly be myself and show the world who I was inside. I can't really say I knew what being gay was all about growing up, even though I had participated in homosexual experiences. All I knew was that everyone thought it was wrong, and even though I enjoyed those experiences, I felt guilty afterwards.

I was, however, always close to the women in my family: my cousins, aunts and my grandmother. They were the majority of my family who did the nurturing and the raising of the children. Growing up I had four moms. My Aunt Pam, who was my mother's oldest sister, and the "leader." All her younger sisters emulated her. Then there was my Auntie Kate. She was the most knowledgeable. Aunt Kate was the first sister to get pregnant, but she was the most responsible. I have asked myself: was this because she had a child at a young age which forced her to be responsible, or was she just born that way? I guess you can say I admired her the most because she always seemed to have her life on track through it all. You never knew, however, what a person was really going through unless they told you. And she never had.

I remembered getting suspended for three days in Middle school for fighting. I didn't know what my grandmother was doing at the time. She was probably in the hospital because she had several nervous break-downs and was hospitalized for weeks and sometimes months as I grew up. If my grandmother had been around, I probably would have stayed at home and watched television during the time-off. But for whatever reason I was staying with my Aunt Kate and she took me to class with her.

At the time she was working full-time at night, and going to school at the University of Washington during the day, which was one of the best universities in the Pacific Northwest.

She'd taken me to her Sociology class that day. The hall had at least 500 students in it. She explained to me that it was a lecture, and on alternating days during the week the courses were broken down to about twenty-five students to a classroom, taught by students working on graduate degrees. The graduate students explained and elaborated on concepts discussed in lecture and also administered and graded homework assignments for the course.

That day I couldn't believe the professor called me down in the front of the lecture hall and used me in one of his demonstrations. I cannot remember exactly what the demonstration was about; all I knew was that this visit to the University of Washington was life-changing for me, and I knew from there I was going to college. I just knew. And the funny thing about the situation was that I was in that same lecture hall when I attended the University of Washington almost five years later.

My Aunt Theresa, making our way down the line of sisters, was a year younger then my mother. She was like my buddy and pal; she would talk to me and treat me like I was an adult. I can honestly say Auntie Theresa was my first best friend. I am talking about a friend who knew you, knew you better than you knew yourself at times.

Then there was my Auntie Peggy who was the baby. Her tactic of survival was stealing. She felt like what she didn't have she could take. It started off with small things like pens and paper from school. Then it escalated to high-time fraud—stealing from major department stores and returning items for cash or store credit—so she could buy things for herself and her children. I would say my Aunt Peggy was the materialistic one of the group. She always appeared to have her life on track, even with the stealing; she managed to keep herself out of trouble. I did know of maybe one or two occasions in which she got caught and went to jail, but not for long. When I was younger I used to babysit her kids for her. I didn't really like babysitting, but this provided me an outlet to be away from home.

After my mother died, I sometimes stayed with my little brother's father, when my grandmother was out of town or had things going on. My brother's father seemed to always have some different woman around me and my brother. I was always afraid of him because he was the disciplinarian; he was the one who gave out the "whuppings." I still could picture Saturday mornings when I wanted to watch cartoons and he wanted to watch sports and I was upset and started crying. "Go get the belt," he would say, and I would have to stick out my hands and he would beat the palm of my hands with a belt. I wouldn't dare move my hands out the way or that would mean more licks. I hated that so much that I would try to avoid him as much as possible. It seemed like I would always make him upset. I thought most kids got spankings on their butt, legs and arms, but not me. I would hate to get "whuppings" but I seemed to always get them, and the reason I would get whuppings was because he thought I was too soft. He would always shout, "Stop crying," or, "You better not cry or I am getting the belt." It got to the point where I did not want to come home after school; I even signed up for after-school sports so I wouldn't have to be in the house with him. He was so mean, and he was so much bigger than I was at the time. He was 6'1, about 185 lbs., real nice build and cut up, because of the type of work he did. He worked for the City of Seattle Sanitation Department as a trash man. Although this work was dirty and grimy, it paid a nice salary. I remembered he'd always dressed well, had a nice car, always a Cadillac, freshly washed on the weekends and he kept money in his pocket and mine too.

He was also able to keep money in his pocket because he usually dated women that took care of him and us, and had better paying jobs than he did. He was considered a ladies' man around town. My mother, before she got on drugs, was very intelligent and athletic, and had a scholarship to play basketball down south, where she met my father.

I was a lot like my mother when she was younger, besides her being blinded by love and on drugs. She was a very talented woman she excelled in school, and was an excellent artist. I still can't figure out what it was or what happened to my mother that made her want to give up everything that she'd accomplished to live a life of despair and sadness. I was too young at the time to really see what my mother was going through. I guess when you're a child you can only see things in one dimension. When it was directly in front of you, but you're too young and naive to really know what was going on behind the fighting and the breakups. To me it was a good and a bad thing, because I was too young to understand the pain. Now that I was an adult, I felt like I needed answers to free myself from my past. I didn't know if I would truly be able to forgive and forget without knowing what my mother was going through that made her life turn out the way it did. I think there was something deeper that made a person addicted to drugs, in a way that it almost made it impossible for them to come back to reality.

It had been a while now since my mother's death and I had become immune to the pain and suffering. However when I was thinking about family or watching something on television that triggered past memories, I always wondered what life would have been like for my brother and me if my mom never started using drugs. I would never know the answer to that question (but I thanked God every day for every opportunity that I've had in life so far).

I THINK THAT I HAD ALWAYS been attracted to men. Some may say it was because I didn't have a strong male presence growing up, but I didn't know if that was totally the case. My brother wasn't gay and most of the men in my family had fathers who were less involved in their lives than my stepfather was in mine. My brother's father did the best he knew how when he was around. He came from a bad and fatherless background and really didn't put forth the effort that my mom, brother and I expected. But now that I was older, I realized that just because you made a baby didn't mean you knew what it was that you were supposed to do to take care of it. And unfortunately there were a lot of black men out here who didn't have a clue.

So I'd finally met up with Tamara, Felicia's roommate. Of course she walked right up to me. "Dontae I am Tee, Felicia's roommate. You look just like your yearbook picture minus the braces." I was relieved because she seemed very friendly. She also had a slight southern accent. She was about 5'3, 125 lbs., small and petite, sporting one of those Halle Berry signature short hairstyles. We clicked instantly. I could tell she was flirting with me. I wasn't really messing with guys all that much in high school, or at least nobody other than the select few guys I had experimented with. So Felicia didn't really know that I was exclusively dating men now (although I am sure she assumed, just like so many other people from my high school). It wasn't that I was flamboyant like they try and portray us in the media, who flaunt their sexual orientation to the world, but I had to be honest, I did have my ways.

I was a perfectionist and as much as I tried not to let it show, it was hard for me to hide it. I cared a lot about the way I looked. I thought your outer appearance was what people saw most, and what you were judged on first. Therefore, I tried to make sure that my outer appearance was always clean and orderly. I got my hair cut weekly. I even had a barber kit at home because two days after getting my hair cut I was touching it up until my next appointment. I made sure my nails were manicured. I had the metro-sexual look way before it became a fad for celebrities and straight men who dressed contemporary. I'd mostly hung around girls in high school too. It just seemed like I had more in common or we were like-minded. What kept some of the students guessing about my sexuality, however, was that I dated a girl named Tiffany all throughout high school. I would never admit to being a down-low brother, I would just say I was confused because I deeply wanted to be straight, and I had no idea that I would later decide to date guys exclusively. I just thought it was a phase that I was going through. Boy was I wrong. I didn't judge anyone. I just couldn't be a part of the secretiveness of the down-low lifestyle; my conscience wouldn't allow me to carry on that lifestyle.

I was tall, very athletic and by most people's standards fairly attractive. So the opposite sex was very interested in trying to figure me out. Most just thought I was quiet and innocent and extremely nice. The people who called me faggot and sissy were the haters. Mainly the boys who were mad because girls paid more attention to me, and the girls who were mad because I wouldn't give them the time of day. I would later find out that the boys who secretly wanted to have sex with me, were the ones doing all the yapping.

"I was thinking we head over to Ben's Chili Bowl to get a bite to eat, before we head back to our place and drop your things off," Tamara said.

"That sounds good to me, I heard about Ben's Chili Bowl, it's s'pose to be real good food, but greasy, I am down for that," I replied back trying to act all street.

"Yeah it is one of my favorite spots to eat in D.C. I have been coming here since I was a freshman at Howard. My girls and I would leave the club at three in the morning and head over there after we worked up a sweat on the dance floor. I always take people who have never been to D.C. to this restaurant because it is like a must-eat-at spot. Plus I never want to miss an opportunity to get my grub on either." We both laughed, but I was extremely hungry from the long eight hour flight.

Ben's Chili Bowl turned out to be fantastic. We'd decided to eat inside and talked to get better acquainted. Tamara worked as an administrative director for an international organization that administered the Fulbright Scholar Program, which gave scholarships and fellowships to college students around the country who wanted to study abroad. The organization was heavily funded by the U.S. Department of State and many colleges and universities around the world. She also mentioned that she'd just broken up with her boyfriend about a month ago, because she suspected that he was cheating on her. Tamara and Felicia started out being roommates while they were in college. They both moved out when they graduated to live with their boyfriends – well actually, Tamara moved out of the apartment, and Felicia's boyfriend moved in. Both relationships didn't work out. It had been a month since Tamara had been back in the apartment. Felicia's boyfriend had been gone for more than six months though.

When we got to their apartment I was shocked at how small it was. It was a basement apartment below a row house, close to the Capitol. When you walked in, the kitchen and the living room were both connected with no separation other than a transition strip separating the carpet in the living room from the vinyl tile in the kitchen. After you passed the kitchen there was a short hallway that ended with a full bath, and on each side there was a bedroom. Felicia's on the right and Tamara's on the left. Tamara said that I could put my things in the closet in the living room. She then showed me the bathroom and both rooms and said that this was it, small and cozy.

I'd never really seen a two-bedroom apartment this small in my life. Their apartment was no more than 900 square feet, and many studios in Seattle were that size. There weren't any basement apartments or row houses in Seattle. We usually called them townhomes, but they were located in the suburbs, not really in the city. I wasn't going to complain about my new living environment. At least I had a place to stay, and Felicia told me that they paid around $1,400 a month for this apartment, so I was sure on my budget I would probably be getting something a lot smaller than this for now. I was guessing I could probably pay $1,000 a month with my scholarship and the money I had saved. I really wanted to meet someone in law school who either needed a roommate or was looking for a roommate to cut down on costs.

I arrived a little less than a week before school started so I could get acquainted with my surroundings. Get used to the time zone change and see if I could have a little fun before I hit the books hard. Now that I was here, I was glad that I came early. I really wanted to check out what all the hype was that I'd been hearing about before I dived head first into law school. I heard the first year in law school was the most demanding year and the grades you got determined what internships you were awarded. It ultimately determined if you would be asked to join some of the top law firms in the country. But first I needed to check out the sites, meet some new people and have a good time. I'd been working all summer trying to save money to move to D.C. so I didn't have a chance to really enjoy the fact that I'd just graduated from college. I was one step away from my goal of becoming a lawyer, so I needed to have some enjoyment because from what I heard, law school was no joke.

Since it was a Friday afternoon, Tee said that she would let me get settled and I could take a nap, then we would head to a party out in Bowie for one of her friends, Jameeka. She had just bought a townhouse and was having a house warming. She explained to me that Bowie was a suburb outside of the city where you would find large homes and yards, which were hard to find in the city. She said many of her friends who she went to school with opted to leave the city for the suburbs, such as Bowie, Fort Washington, Clinton, Waldorf and Accokeek where they could get more house for their money and start raising families. She explained to me that Jameeka was a teacher in P.G. County and had graduated from Howard with her and Felicia. She also said the party was going to be really nice and would be a good chance for me to meet people. I was game to going to the party even though I was kind of tired since I didn't get any sleep on the plane ride. I was too busy anticipating my arrival and all the things I would do and how my new life in D.C. would unfold.

I FELL ASLEEP ON THE COUCH and woke up when I heard Felicia come through the front door. She looked just like she did when we were in high school plus about twenty pounds that looked really good on her. I was sure the guys in D.C.

were all over that body, she now had a nice round booty, shapely thick thighs and voluptuous breasts. She used to e-mail me that ever since she'd been in D.C. she'd been addicted to collard greens, macaroni and cheese, fried chicken and pork chops, things she really didn't eat growing up in Seattle. Back home, the only time she would be able to enjoy these types of foods was during the holidays. Now that she lived in D.C., a lot of folks from the south (where the food was said to have originated from) had moved up here and she would get her share of soul food almost every Sunday.

Looking at her I could see that it had caught up with her in a sexy way. You could describe her figure as having that classic "hour glass" shape. "Hey Dontae, you look great, let me look at you to make sure you are still my friend that I knew way back when," Felicia laughed. She'd given me a strong hug and spun me a round in three hundred sixty degrees. "Yeah, that's you, how you been?"

"I've been good, excited to see you after all these years. It's still hard to believe I just picked up and left. I thought I would be in Seattle forever. I never thought I would have the guts to just leave and start all over again. Of course you are here to make it easier, but I know we haven't seen each other in years except for your occasional visits to see your family. I know you have a life, friends and a whole new out look on life since I knew you. I plan to get my place as soon as possible, so you can go back to your life, and we can see how we fit into each others lives," I said. By this time we were sitting on the couch. She was looking at me and I was looking at her, we were trying to get a glimpse of the person we knew but didn't really know anymore, which was a paradox, I think.

"Well do what you feel you need to feel comfortable, I will be here if you need me," she replied. "Well let me go get into the shower, I am sure I smell like the ocean and salt, all the crabs I ate today. I know Tee told you about the party. We should be leaving in like an hour or so." She hugged me and walked into her room after turning on the shower. I guess that was my cue to start figuring out what I was wearing to the party because it was almost time to go.

I already had in my backpack what I was wearing for such an occasion. I knew we were going out somewhere. I thought it would be a restaurant or a club for my first night, but a house party – wow. I was having a hard time not feeling like this was a welcome party for me, even though it wasn't. I guess it's just the excitement in me that I was about to mix and mingle on the east coast. I had in my bag a pair of jeans I bought from Macy's; the name brand was Lucky. Lucky jeans seemed to fit me real nice. I was tall and had thick thighs and a big butt for a guy and for some reason Lucky was the brand that I could always find something that would fit me nicely. Even though my waist was somewhere between a thirty and thirty-two, I usually had to buy a thirty-four because smaller-size jeans fit too tight around my thigh area. I had a hard time finding jeans and it sucked because I wished I could walk into a Banana Republic or Gap and find me a pair, like most people, but I rarely did. The shirt that I picked out was a black short-sleeved collared shirt, with creases about two inches apart coming down the shirt, by a designer out of Seattle, Kenny Clemmons. He was a really good friend of mine and I hoped he made it big-time because he could design his ass off. I also had my Kenneth Cole loafers in the bag as well.

My style was pretty basic, but very up-to-date, I didn't do too much with clothes and I didn't wear flamboyant colors. I liked the polished put-together look. I had just got my hair cut before I left from my younger cousin who was a barber/entrepreneur. He usually hooked me up with a fresh fade once a week, sometimes every other week. Now that I was in D.C., I was going to have to find a barber who could cut my hair just as good if not better than my cousin.

When Felicia had finished her shower, she yelled to me that I could use the bathroom to get ready. So I took out my toiletry bag with my deodorant, toothbrush, wave cap, grease and brush and headed to their small bathroom that only had a shower, toilet and vanity. I took a shower so I could wash away the funk and sweat from my flight from. When I finished up in the bathroom I saw that they had the iron set up in the living room. I took it upon myself to iron my shirt so that too could be fresh since it was folded in my back pack for all those hours. When it was time for us to leave I sprayed some Polo Sport on as the finishing touch to my outfit and I dashed out the door with two fine sisters on my arms. They both had on real low shorts that stopped about two inches past the crotch. Felicia had on all white ones with a sleeveless yellow rayon shirt that went slightly past her waist and Tamara had on kaki-colored ones with a green sleeveless cotton shirt on that just went past her waist. They looked like they were dancers for Destiny's Child walking out of the apartment.

We decided to take Felicia's truck since it was newer and nicer than Tamara's 1991 Honda CRX, which would have been too small for us to fit in anyway. Felicia had the new Toyota RAV4 which she was excited about driving.

When we arrived to the townhouse in Bowie I could tell we were at the right place because balloons were streaming from the porch and there was a couple outside with drinks in hand smoking cigarettes. They turned to look at us as we walked up to the party.

"Hey, Rita and Keith!" Tamara said as she recognized the couple. They immediately left each other's side and gave Tamara and Felicia a hug. Then Felicia introduced me as a friend from high school and they both gave me a handshake. Rita told us everyone else was inside eating and fixing drinks and they would be inside in a few minutes. That was the cue for us to give them some more privacy and we gladly took the cue to see what was on the other side of the door where the loud music was playing.

There were several people in the home, sitting and standing, talking to people. Everyone had a drink in-hand; some also had appetizer plates filled with fried chicken and pasta salad. When you walked into the house you could see the whole first level. As soon as you walked in you had to walk up to the living room area, where there was a couch, a love seat, and a recliner all made of a dark brown micro fiber, which invited you into the cozy place. The whole first level was covered with hardwood floors and area rugs placed neatly in a decorative fashion.

The living room design was a combination dining room, where there was a six-person dining room table, with catered food in aluminum pans covered with foil that folks were standing near. Finally the kitchen was at the back of the house that had a sliding glass door leading to a deck the size of the living room. There was a really nice vibe; it seemed like everyone was young and happy, experiencing life for all the joy that each day brings. Little did I or they know that our lives were just beginning and nothing in life was ever perfect. Hopefully we would make some good choices along the way because the only guarantee in this world was one day we would all die, and as much as we wanted to think we knew, nobody really knew what happened after life was over. Was there a heaven where we would feel content like this all the time, and we would never run into heartbreak, neglect or jealousy? I damn sure hoped so! But a new chapter in my life was starting and boy was I ready to see it unfold.

CHAPTER 3

J.P.

I had nothing but a blast since being in D.C., but it was now time to be serious. Law school orientation started in two hours and I couldn't wait to see what classes I was going to have and meet all the new students. I decided to wear my gray business suit with the black silk slip that hung about an inch below that looked real cute on me. I decided to put my hair in a slicked-back ponytail with a black rubber band, which made me look real professional. I knew I wanted to be there about thirty minutes before so I could see everyone walking into the building. And since I hadn't gone grocery shopping to buy my morning coffee yet, I needed to stop by Starbucks and grab a Grande Latté.

When I got to Georgetown's law school, I found parking in the student lot near the library and headed inside. The auditorium where the orientation was being held was near where I parked, and there were signs with arrows directing first-year students to where they needed to go. When I arrived inside, there were about 20 students that had already gotten there, and there was only one other black person there so far which was a guy. He was standing near the front near the stage right in the center where the podium was. I could tell he was excited to be here; he probably didn't get any sleep last night just like me. He was cute, and tall. "Redbone," I thought to myself. When I introduced myself to him, I was kind of shocked because we both had the same green eyes. I had met people with green eyes before, but some had a hazel tint, and others had brown circles around them. His and mine, though, were the same, and the only person I knew with the same hue as mine was my mother. The three of us had light green eyes in the middle of our pupils and the outside of our pupils leading to the whites of our eyes were a different shade of green, a darker shade. I wondered to myself could me and this guy be related.

"Hi, my name is Jennifer; by the way you're dressed and standing right here in front of the podium I know you are a 1-L, just like me," I said shaking the unknown guy's hand. 1-L is what they called a first-year law student.

"Yeah I guess I am that obvious. I have been here for an hour waiting for orientation to get started," he said, kind of embarrassed. I reassured him that he wasn't the only one, and I couldn't get any sleep last night anticipating this day. He confessed he hadn't gotten any sleep either and was wired from drinking three cups of coffee before getting to school. He introduced himself as Dontae and said that he was originally from Seattle and this was his first time in Washington. As he was talking I couldn't help but assume he was gay, and it wasn't because he was flamboyant or even feminine. It was just that he never looked down at my breast or even gave me the impression that he was sizing me up while he was talking to me. The conversation was natural and real, and being from Atlanta, I had met my share of gay men, and this was usually how our conversations went.

He was very outgoing and that made me feel comfortable. Most men never showed women that initial vulnerability he conveyed. Most men that I ran across would be acting all hard, grabbing their crotches acting like "yeah, I got this," even though it was the first day, and they were probably as nervous as I was, if not more. I appreciated that Dontae was so open and I knew we would be friends from that moment on. Once the auditorium started to fill up there were about thirty or so other black students at the orientation. I didn't meet anyone else that day other than faculty because Dontae and I decided to use this time to get to know each other. Once the orientation was over we picked up our schedules, and noticed that we had all the same courses and decided to head over to the bookstore together to purchase our books.

Dontae had taken a cab to school and informed me that he was staying with a friend from high school who lived in the area until he could find a place of his own. I could tell that Dontae wasn't rich nor did he have a father like me who could afford my apartment, car, tuition and books. Dontae was on a scholarship and had financial aid. In the bookstore he used a voucher that the school had given him to purchase his books. I used the AMEX card that my father paid for every month. Dontae kind of reminded me of Kenya and so many other black students that I met at Spelman who were on financial aid. They didn't have cars and lived in houses with several roommates because they couldn't afford to live alone. I respected these students very much because they had ambition to strive to be better than where they came from. It was okay that their parents never went to college or that there were no doctors or lawyers in their family. It didn't stop them from trying to become doctors, lawyers, and politicians. In some way I felt like them; my mother was smart, when she was alive, but not educated in the worldly sense and my father was a self-proclaimed music mogul.

After we went to the bookstore, we walked around the campus to see where all our classes would be held. It was around noon by the time we finished, and the law school was having a barbecue in front of the library where the new students could mingle. However, Dontae and I decided to skip the barbecue and go out and find a restaurant in the city where we could have lunch and get some drinks. We both figured that we would have three years to meet the rest of the students and D.C. was too new for the both of us and we wanted to explore. We decided to go to an Ethiopian restaurant in the Adams-Morgan section of the city. We both had heard a lot about this part of town. Adams-Morgan is considered the international section of the city. Many bars, clubs and a variety of foreign restaurants were located in that area. We had planned to come back on a weekend and see what the nightlife was all about.

After we ate, I dropped Dontae off where he was staying around three p.m., and we'd planned to hook back up and see more of the city around eight p.m. His sexuality never came up and I wanted to ask him, but I thought it would be rude and ruin the mood that we'd established so I left it alone. I expected if we hung out together for some time he would open up and let me know, and I firmly believed in respecting privacy. Shit he was real sexy and I knew most people thought we were a couple while we were hanging out. I kind of didn't mind. It wasn't that I'd wanted him to be my man or anything. It was just that I haven't really had any male companionship in some time and Dontae had made me feel special. It was like he cared what I had to say and appreciated my opinion. Most men just talked over you and tried to run game, or at least that was what my experience with most men had been so far.

I was sure daddy had a lot to do with the way I felt about guys and that's why it was hard for me to get close to someone. I just felt that most men were dogs and got bored easily with women. They would have the most attractive women in their lives willing to do whatever they wanted. Some women changed who they were for their men, but that still wasn't enough. How did you explain Eric Benet cheating on someone like Halle Berry? I mean she adopted his daughter, confessed her love to him to the whole world and he still cheated. He blamed it on having a sex addiction, which I think was completely bullshit. Love should've been enough to get over any addiction.

The problem was that men, and especially black men, didn't realize what they had until it was gone. Also, black men who had a little bit going on for themselves knew that they were a hot commodity and used this as an advantage to sleep with and manipulate as many women as they could.

I didn't want to be one of those women who wasted her youth with a man who didn't appreciate her. I refused to be *that* girl who spent her youth running over backwards for a no-good man. When she got into her late thirties or early forties he left her for the fastest young thing smoking. This was my fear, which had made it hard for me to trust men. I knew I didn't like women, so I knew I was going to have to get over that before I could meet the right guy. I was hoping since I was living in the nation's capital, where there were supposed to be very educated, smart and eligible black men, that I would be able to find that "diamond in the rough." Maybe I would be able to settle down and have a few kids. I had to believe there were some good black men in the world who weren't gay or married.

Growing up I'd always thought that life would be so much different for me. Thought I would be a professional singer, traveling the world and touching people with my voice. I hadn't thought about singing since my mother died. But seeing Dontae's green eyes brought back memories of her. I missed my mother. Lord knows I did. I wished she'd never left this world. Too bad she didn't pick her life back up like so many people do and find another man, or learned to live by herself. Since my mother died I'd been trying to block a lot of stuff from my mind so I didn't have to think about it, but those eyes were all I could think about at the moment. I knew my mother hadn't come back as Dontae, but I couldn't help but wonder why I met this guy with the same eyes as my mother and me.

I longed to hear that infectious voice one more time, feel her embrace around my body, and hear her tell me that everything was going to be alright. That my father still loved me and so did she. It was this moment I realized that I wasn't hurting anybody but myself by not singing. God had given me a gift and I couldn't let tragedy keep me from my gift. Singing was what I did well and helped me express myself in ways that I couldn't get out any other way but in song. It was a part of me that I had been hiding for so many years, because I didn't want to deal with the pain of losing my mother.

I thought that if I didn't sing I wouldn't think about her. If I didn't sing then I wouldn't cry myself to sleep at night. If I didn't sing then I wouldn't remember that I ever had a mother and I could go on with my life. But that was not true, because I dreamed about her almost every night. It was the same dream over and over again; me, around the age when my father left, holding my favorite cabbage patch doll, saying, "Mommy, why did you leave me too? Have I been a bad, bad girl…?" Before she answered, I would wake up, and so many times I'd tried to close my eyes and get back into that dream awaiting the answer to the question never getting a response.

Now that law school seemed to have gotten off to a good start, I was sure that everything in my life would work itself out. I was going to do my best to open my heart more, learn to be more trusting and forgive my mom for committing suicide. There was a long road to travel for me but I was sure that I could make it in a new city.

It was going to be different for me going to school with boys in my classes. Being at Spelman an all girls' school, there was no added pressure when called upon to answer a question. Girls really didn't threaten me but I remember in high school, when I had to give a presentation or answer a question in class, there was always one boy who made me self-conscious and nervous.

Other women never made me nervous to present or express my ideas. At Spelman, girls didn't feel that we had to be all dolled up with makeup and the latest trends when we went to class. When I would go over to the campuses of Clark-Atlanta and Morris Brown, it was a modern-day fashion show, the girls and the guys both looked like they had just walked off a runway. Another thing I had to get used to was going to school with whites, where blacks were the minority. I knew this would be a whole new ball game for me. I figured since the real world was not all black, going to Georgetown would give me a better idea of what to expect when I got into the workforce.

Some people felt that you didn't get the best education going to an exclusively black college. They still believed that "separate-but-not-equal" campaign used in the early twentieth century so blacks and whites would not be allowed to attend the same schools. I knew that racism still existed in America and many public schools in the black and Latino neighborhoods didn't get the same amount of resources as white neighborhoods. But I felt it was my choice to learn from people like me, get a different perspective on life, when I had a choice. To me there was nothing wrong with choosing to go to an all-black college. School to me is what you learn as an individual. Teaching is like a two-way street. You can have the best or the smartest teacher, but if the student is not in the mind frame for learning, then the student won't learn.

I've had friends who took the same courses as me and we each took different lessons from those courses. I've also had classes with students who passed the course but didn't learn a damn thing. I'd always made it a point to grasp most concepts from each class I took. I liked the challenge of figuring things out, or picking up the lessons that the teacher was trying to get across. Most people viewed me as being a "know-it-all" or a nerd, which wasn't the case at all. I'd just always been the one to do the reading, and take really good notes in all my classes so I could follow along with the professor. What my friends failed to realize was they would be just as smart if they applied themselves. Don't get me wrong, I've had a few classes where I didn't apply myself and my grades reflected as such. The only way I was going to do well was by applying myself.

I decided to stop by the supermarket to get a few things on the way home. I most definitely needed to get some coffee, cream and sugar to get me through the mornings. I also needed to get some other items so that I could make myself some breakfast and have some snacks around the house in case I didn't feel like going out to get something to eat. I was really not the person to have chips, cookies and a lot of snack items around my house. I knew if they were there I would eat them all and I was doing my damnedest to keep my size six figure.

Keeping this figure was hard when fried chicken was your favorite food, among other fattening foods. I really didn't work out all that much, so dieting was the only way for me to maintain my weight. Now that I was in D.C., I was going to join a health club and take some aerobic classes. I'd heard so many times, when you start getting older your metabolism slows down. I wanted to be more than ready when that time came.

The grocery store wasn't packed when I got there, but I did notice that the fruit and vegetables weren't as fresh as what I was used to. I actually heard someone trying to get some fresh tomatoes cursing to herself. "It is a shame how they do us in the black neighborhoods. It makes no sense that I can't find one tomato without something growing on the side of it or it looking all jacked up. I bet you if I was out in Virginia or in Georgetown the vegetables would be a lot fresher." I agreed with a nod. She was right; this was ridiculous. We paid with the same kind of money that the white folks paid with; why did our food have to be of less quality? So I bypassed the fresh fruit and vegetable section and got a few items that would get me through the weekend, because I planned on doing my shopping elsewhere.

When I got home I put away the few groceries that I bought and checked my voicemail, which let me know that I had three messages. The first one was from daddy, wishing me good luck and letting me know he was sorry he didn't catch me before I went into orientation. He told me he was really proud of me and would talk to me and see me soon. He reminded me that he had to do some radio promotions for some new artists in D.C. the following week and he wanted to get together and take me out to eat and show me some places that he frequented when he comes down. I couldn't wait for this to happen because spending time with daddy was one of my favorite things to do. It made me feel like a little girl again and he still treated me like I was only seven sometimes.

The second message was from Kenya. She wanted to see how my orientation went and asked if we could go grab something to eat if I didn't have anything to do later.

"I did have something to do but I wondered if it would be alright if you joined me and my new friend Dontae," I thought to myself as her message ended.

The last and final message was from Dontae. "Well, I wanted to thank you for making my first day go by so smoothly, as promised here is my cell phone number, 206-555-1212, so we can get together later on tonight, which I am really looking forward to doing. Anyway, talk to you later. It was a pleasure meeting you Jennifer, I mean J.P.," Dontae laughed as he hung up the phone.

After I listened to the messages I turned on the TV to fuzz which reminded me that the cable guy would be here on Saturday between the hours of 8:00 a.m. and 12:00 p.m. He would most likely arrive closer to the later part of the window, which had always happened to me when it came to getting my cable installed. I decided to pop in my graduation DVD, not because I wanted to watch it, but because it was the only DVD that I had that was nearby. Not soon after I turned it on, I was in a silent nap dreaming about my future, and to my surprise it was not a nightmare, although I didn't remember much of it when I woke up.

I DIDN'T SLEEP AS LONG as I thought I was going to. I guess I wasn't as tired as I thought or I was just too excited to be in bed. So I grabbed my cell phone and dialed Dontae to see what he was up to.

"Hey Dontae, this is J.P. I was calling to see if we were still going to hook up this evening, I was thinking I would pick you up at 8:30?"

"Hey how are you, J.P.? I was just telling my friends I am staying with all about you. I didn't even get any rest, I been on the computer looking for places around the school," he replied. "Anyway, 8:30 sounds perfect, have you decided what you wanted to do besides explore the city?"

"Well, kind of, my sorority sister from Spelman lives here and she said something about going somewhere tonight, so I am calling to see if you thought we should all hang out?"

"Yeah that sounds good, since she knows the city and all," Dontae said.

"Well now that is set, let me get off the phone get ready and call Kenya back and I should be there to pick you up around 8:30 or so."

"Sounds like a plan, see ya later," and he hung the phone up.

I then scrolled down to my phone contacts and called Kenya to set everything up. She said she would be at my spot around eight and she knew of a nice place where we could eat, have a few drinks and it turned into a club for dancing later. She thought that they had a comedy show that night.

I didn't really care what I did. Classes started in another three days and I really didn't have anything else to do, plus I couldn't wait until Kenya met Dontae. I was sure she'd get a kick out of meeting him just like I did. I took about a five-minute shower just to make sure that I'd checked that those "not-so-easy-to-touch places" still smelled fresh. I hated to go any place hungry, so I ate some pretzels and drank a beer and then brushed my teeth before Kenya got here. I was so glad I picked up a six-pack of Coronas at the store, so Kenya could have something to drink while I finished getting ready.

I turned my stereo on and started listening to Mary J. Blige's "Share My World" album which was my favorite CD from the queen of hip hop. I didn't know if it was the time of my life when the CD came out – I was having the most fun in my life – or it was just that damn good. I didn't know, all I knew was ever since this CD came out Mary had been on top of the charts but I still hadn't felt her as much as this particular CD, although I loved me some Mary. I was going to spend the time I had left before Kenya got here doing my hair, since I had it slicked in a pony tail all day giving Georgetown "America's Next Black Business Woman." I needed to get back to looking like I was a real sister, or at least look like my mother taught me how to do my hair. I wrapped my hair before I took a nap. I still wanted to straighten it a little more so I turned on the flat iron, and of course the curling iron. I was so glad I came a week early so I could organize and unpack my apartment because everything looked real cute in its place, I had even put in a bookcase that I bought at IKEA so I could store all my books that I would be using for school; you never knew when you wanted to reference back.

By eight o'clock I managed to iron the shirt and jeans that I was wearing tonight and my hair was done. I just needed to spray it with some ultra sheen, slip on my clothes and I was ready to go. When I was done spraying my hair I heard a knock on the door.

"Hey girl, you look nice and I love those micro braids, I am going to have to try those soon," I said to Kenya as I opened up the front door wearing my robe. Her braids were light brown and the roots of her hair were braided tight and small. The rest of the fake hair was left unbraided and was long. I loved the style.

"I see things never change you still take forever to get ready and you don't mind having folks waiting on your butt," she laughed and gave me a hug.

"Well I will be ready in a few minutes I just need to slip on my clothes. There is beer in the refrigerator that you can sip on while you're waiting. So what's new in your world?"

"Girl, the same ole' nonsense at work! These racist white folks paying us these low-ass wages. Sending well-qualified black people on menial assignments, knowing they are over-qualified. They're saving the long-term assignments for the white folks that come in the door with hardly a high school diploma. I cannot wait until I start my own company because

I am tired of being labeled the militant black girl, just for trying to give my people good paying jobs. Their mission is, 'a well equipped workforce for today's diverse challenges, with the right people to give you the competitive edge.' I mean do they even know what diverse means? Girl, I can go on-and-on about my life, which is work and school at this point, which is why I am glad you are here. Maybe I can start enjoying myself like we use to do. Honey, you use to always help me get the stress out my body and you never had to massage any part of it."

"Girl, you know what you have to do, if you're passionate about finding jobs for people in our community, then you need to open up your own business doing just that. I mean you have all the experience working at that temporary agency you've been working for the last eight months and you told me yourself it isn't rocket science."

"That is true, girl, and you know that is my dream, you know I am going to make it happen if it breaks me, but I am already broke from all these school loans I am going to have to pay back for this master's in human resources I am getting."

"I am so jealous that you have a purpose and that you know what you want to do with your life." I had finally put all my clothes on. I was thinking that my homegirl really was amazing. She had purpose in her life that would make her successful. By doing so would help a lot of people out in the process and she wasn't even thinking about being successful, just helping people that needed a little help in life.

It was 8:20 when we pulled out of my crib. We decided to take my car since it was new, and not the two-seater that Cordel bought her when they were still dating. When I looked at the car, she saw that I was shocked because she still owned it.

"Girl this car is paid off and it was in my name when I left his ass, including a ten-year extended warranty that he paid for up front. Love is blind but I am not stupid!" Kenya said as she hopped in my truck. And I wasn't mad at her for that, even considering the circumstances, but it wasn't her fault they broke up and the car was kick ass.

We picked up Dontae and headed to the club that Kenya directed me to. It was packed when we got there. We had to stand outside in line for at least thirty minutes before we got in. The only reason we got in as soon as we did was because Kenya saw a guy she knew working security. This was definitely not what we were used to in Atlanta where we were VIP, but I guess I had to stake my claim to this city like I knew how to do. Kenya knew this cute security guard because she helped him get a job in the security department of a large government contracting firm in the area.

He noticed Kenya in line and said. "There is no way I am going to let you and your friends stand in line, after hooking a brother up so nicely." He also whispered in her ear and I overheard, "I now have my three kids on my insurance plan, which reduces my child support payments. Ja-kwan is not even spending my hard-earned money on my kids. I have to take them shopping every time I see them because she has them looking a mess, which is why I am working here part time. I still need money for my new wife, Aquanisha, and she is expecting a baby girl in three months."

Kenya just smiled and said thank you and wished the man luck with the baby and family. She also whispered in my ear that her job was more than just finding jobs it was actually giving them advice on how to deal with life, and its setbacks. As well as being an ear for listening to the many problems that her clients were going through.

The three of us got into the club a little after nine, and it was a two-level cozy and contemporary spot. When you walked into the club the downstairs contained a bar to the left and a sitting area, so as you waited on your drink you could look out the window and see what was going on outside. If you walked about ten feet past this area there was a larger bar situated on the left-hand wall and directly across from the bar there was a buffet table. The buffet line was wrapped around the corner. Then as you passed the second bar area, there were tables set up in a dining room area, where you could order food, which had a small makeshift bar set off in the corner. I was kind of shocked by everything that was packed in this small space on the first floor.

There were four people getting up from one of the tables as we walked in the dining area, so we decided to ask the waitress to clean the area and asked for menus. The waitress asked us if we wanted to put an order in at the bar before she came back to take our order, and all three of us looked at each other and blurted out yes at the same time, giggling.

"I see you ladies like to drink, that means we have all something in common already," Dontae blurted out. "Let the ladies order first."

"I will have a Long Island Ice Tea," Kenya said ordering first.

"And I will have a Mai Tai, and can you make that a double with no ice?" I asked.

"And I will take a vodka and cranberry," Dontae said right after me.

So the waitress asked Dontae, "Hey, did you want me to make that a double for you too?"

"No, I want to pace myself, but thanks for asking."

"Hey, can you do me a favor and save our spots? This is their first time here and I want to show them the upstairs while we are waiting on our drinks. We will be right back, probably before you get back with the drinks," Kenya said.

"Sure, and welcome to Club Fierce, you two. I am Tiffany; I also want to let you know that the comedy show will start in about an hour upstairs, so I will try to have your food out in enough time for you to enjoy the show."

Everyone said thank you in unison and Dontae and I followed Kenya up the back steps near the dining area where we were sitting. Upstairs was somewhat designed just like the downstairs, minus the dining room. As soon as you walked up the steps you could tell this was the dance floor, because of the fresh clean hardwood floors. At the end of the dance floor there was an elevated stage and in the corner you could see the DJ booth. They had a mic set up and there were high tables and chairs dispersed along the dance floor for folks to sit once the show started. As you walked toward the front part of the club upstairs there were bars and couches placed in the same areas as they were downstairs. Upstairs there were more people drinking and socializing with one another.

When we got back downstairs Tiffany was just sitting our drinks down on the table, "here are your drinks, and I hope you liked the club. I will be right back to take your orders. Since this is your first time coming you two, let me tell you that our crab cakes are excellent."

"Thank you again," we all said in unison.

"I never tried crab cakes before," Dontae said.

"Oh really," Kenya said. "Are you serious? Isn't Seattle near the Pacific Ocean? I would think you would have tasted all kinds of seafood platters. Anyway, you are in for a treat! It's just crab meat, with seafood seasoning onions and breaded cake. It's excellent, especially here."

"Oh, I think I am going to try the crab cakes. I always enjoy crab cakes, and I am glad you are trying crab cakes for the first time with me. Now I know we will be friends for a while," I said. I was kind of tipsy from the cocktails and I didn't know why I said that, but I did want Dontae to know that I was glad to meet him and I really did hope we would be friends for a while because he was such a nice guy. You could tell that it wasn't just an act; I never met a man like him before, gay or straight. He also was very attractive to the eye and I knew most women and men thought the same. Even if you preferred dark-skinned men over light-skinned men, you would have to find Dontae adorable.

We ended up ordering two orders of their crab cakes, an order of their Cajun green beans and chicken wings so we could all share. We decided since we would be getting our drink on tonight that we would fill up with grease to make sure we didn't get too tipsy and leave with some fine man we saw in the club. Or at least that is what Kenya and I was thinking; I was still not sure about Dontae.

When our food came out and we talked about what we all wanted to accomplish in the future. Kenya talked about her starting her own employment agency and Dontae told us that he planned to work for the district attorney's office in a major city to help him pay back his student loans. He then hopefully practiced law for three years for a top law firm in New York, L.A. or San Francisco. He hoped open up his own firm later, or maybe even run for state office. So everyone was enjoying themselves and talking and drinking and I couldn't believe I told them I was going to start singing again, and maybe join a band.

I really wanted to sing again and I had to tell somebody. It amazed me that I just blurted it out. But shit, since they all had exciting things to report I needed to have something too. And as soon as I said that, all the attention went to me. Kenya had known I used to sing, and she was around when I decided to stop singing. She looked at me like she had just seen a ghost. She always said I had made a rash decision. And I knew I did as well but all I could think about when my mom died was how much she used to love to sing. And during that time in my life I thought my singing needed to die with her. But, I'd realized that now with my singing my mom would live on through me.

Kenya was more than delighted to hear that I planned to start singing again and Dontae was excited that I could sing. He said he loved music and would sing to himself all his favorite music every time he had a chance to. It wasn't enough to just be around people who had a purpose for their own lives. The real quencher for me was to make sure that their ambition and determination spilled over onto me and made me want to do something positive. I needed to make my own dent in the world. I couldn't live my life through other people. Shit, I was special too. I had a light that needed to shine just as bright as anyone else's. Having thought of something to live for and give myself purpose, I started feeling better about myself and glad that I moved to D.C. and got back in contact with Kenya.

After we ate and had a few more cocktails we went upstairs to watch the comedy show. When we got upstairs the comedy show was just beginning and there was this local comedian on stage by the name of Rayford Jones. The announcer said we would be in for a treat, because Rayford tore the house down at several spots in D.C. and had been on Russell Simmons' Def Comedy Jam.

When Rayford came to the stage he was a heavy-set brown-skinned guy, with a Marc Ecko sweatsuit on. He looked a lot more casual than everyone else in the room who were all dressed to impress. The DJ was right; Rayford was hilarious. Everyone in the room was cracking up laughing as soon as he hit the stage until he was finished. The three of us were sitting at a table near the front, and just before Rayford got off the stage he pointed to Dontae and said, "Look at that light-skin dude with the two fine ladies beside him. I don't know, but those two look like the finest ladies I seen all day. Don't tell me they are both yours; you ain't that lucky are you playa?" Everyone in the audience started laughing. "Anyway, management wanted me to tell you and everyone else sitting at these tables as soon as I leave the stage, the tables will be moved out the way and we're going to dance and get this party started until the wee hours of the morning. Just wanted to let y'all know sitting down not to get too comfortable because you're gonna have to get up. Light-skin, if one of your ladies is single maybe we can start the Electric Slide when the music comes on." Dontae was shaking his head with a look of embarrassment. Kenya grabbed him around his shoulders and said it will be okay and started laughing harder.

When the comedian left the stage we and everyone else who was sitting at the tables got up and let the Hispanic workers clear the dance floor. The music was blasting and the DJ was playing Jay-Z and Mya's joint the "Best of Me" which drew everyone to the dance floor. I must admit that this song was hot, but I'd never thought Mya was all that great of a singer when she came out with the popular group Dru Hill.

Kenya and I had drinks that were halfway full, so we went out to the dance floor and Dontae went to the bar to get another drink.

As soon as Dontae left two guys came up to us and said that Rayford was right, that we were the finest women in the club, and asked if we wanted to dance. They were both over six feet tall and well dressed. Kenya and I both gave them a once-over look, looked at each other, and said why not. The guy that grabbed my hand didn't have very much rhythm, but his confidence was high that he didn't too much care that he wasn't moving to the beat. The dance floor got packed. I got into the music and couldn't see where Kenya and her partner were on the dance floor. After about two more songs my drink was pretty much empty and on cue the guy I was dancing with grabbed my hand and led me to the bar.

"Hey pretty lady, it was hard keeping up with you on the dance floor. By the way, my name is Mark Lewis. I see that you can use another drink; what can I get for you?"

"Oh thank you, you're right. I am sitting here babysitting an empty drink. By the way my name is Jennifer Peale, but most people just call me J.P. for short. I was drinking a Mai Tai, and I would love another one."

"Jennifer, well I would like to call you Jennifer if I may, I love that name and it suits you. So do you come here often? I been here several times, since I been in D.C."

"Well actually this is my first time here, and I am having a good time. I just moved here from Atlanta, and already it appears that D.C. is more sophisticated. I mean don't get me wrong, Atlanta is progressive, but it just seems like D.C. is more settled. It's like what Atlanta will be like in a few years."

"Well I think you're right, I am from Houston and I have been to Atlanta to party and visit a lot, and I think the farther north you get the more sophisticated and livelier things are. Anyway, here is your drink," and Mark handed me the fresh cocktail. "I would love to dance with you some more, maybe all that moving and shaking you're doing will rub off on me, and I will look half as good as you do on the dance floor."

"That sounds like a plan, but let me see if I can find my two friends. I will meet you near the dance floor in less than five minutes."

"See you in five, Jennifer."

"Aaight," I said, and went to look for Dontae first and he wasn't hard to find at all; he was standing next to two guys and a girl. He was near the bar at the far end next to the pool table. They looked as if they were having a really interesting conversation. Everyone was looking at the guy standing next to Dontae who had the floor talking about how D.C. had so many places to go and that it was the Mecca for us young, gifted, and talented black youth. "We are doing things that our ancestors could only imagine doing in America, and we should be very proud of ourselves."

I couldn't help but agree and actually realize how far we have come, from slavery to young black kings and queens of our own destiny in life. I waited until he finished his thought before I got Dontae's attention and called him a little closer to me so he could hear me. "I see you met some nice folks, I met this nice guy and we are going to get back on the dance floor. I am just checking to see if you were okay; and I see that you are. So I am going to head back and I will see you in a few. I expect to hear details later."

"Oh ok, get your groove on and I will see you in a lil' bit," Dontae said and we squeezed hands and I walked away.

As soon as I walked away, I spotted Kenya sitting next to the couches near the middle bar with a different guy than when I left her. They were sipping on cocktails and engrossed in conversation. She saw me walking by and signaled to me that she would come find me in a little while. I was kind of happy to see that everyone was enjoying themselves and didn't need me interrupting their groove. So I went to go find the nice gentleman that I had met and stopped playing mommy.

CHAPTER 4

Dontae

It had been such an exhaustive and eventful past two weeks. I'd never imagined I'd hit D.C. as hard as I did in such a short period of time. Things were now winding down for me and for good reason – law school was no joke. I had over five hundred pages of reading a night and I didn't know how these professors expected us to get all this reading and work done and get any sleep or food in the process. I must admit that I'd been quite the social buff since landing in Chocolate City. It had been good though being able to meet some real positive people. J.P. and I were inseparable ever since we met at orientation. We had a lot in common and some of the same sort of values. We got along really well and she was really generous, which was refreshing since I was on a tight budget until I got my reimbursement check from my scholarship. I needed to find a part-time job to supplement my income while I was in school.

J.P. didn't have to work, had her own place, drove a Land Cruiser and even though she had free tuition because of her grades, her father covered her apartment and anything else she needed like books, food, etc. She mentioned to me that he was some music mogul, which made perfect sense when she said that she wanted to pursue singing in her spare time. I was sure if she was as good as her girl Kenya said she was her father could get her a record deal. I mean she more than had the looks, J.P. was a fine sister. It was funny because we both had the same green eyes and since we had all the same classes many of our fellow classmates kept asking us if we were brother and sister.

J.P. had taken me to several places since I met her. We went out to a club the first night, and I ended up meeting some Howard graduate students at the club. I had hit it off with one guy in particular: his name was Jemal, he was getting his MBA from Howard and it just so happened that he was looking for a roommate. He had gone to Howard for undergrad, majored in accounting and worked for fortune-five-hundred company, Ernst and Young, as an auditor for two years before deciding to come back and get his MBA. He said he always knew he wanted to get his master's and he was tired of being flown out from city to city locked in a company's conference room or cubicle trying to locate discrepancies in financial reports and stack billable hours for his company. He said that his roommate had just finished his degree in acting at Howard, and was moving to New York to try his luck in the Big Apple. He really didn't want to have to move into a smaller place and run the risk of maybe having to move to the southeast section of the city where the rent was a lot cheaper, if he couldn't find a reliable roommate.

Of course, I ate all that information up, and mentioned to him that I was looking for a place to stay and would love to check out the place to see if he wouldn't mind having me as a roommate. So he gave me his number and I hung out with him and his two friends George and Brenda for the rest of the night. J.P. and Kenya were nowhere in sight until the club was about to close and the DJ announced last call. On our way home, I told them both about meeting Jemal and the possibility of having a roommate situation that I was going to check out. J.P. told me that would be great and if I needed a ride checking out spots, she would be more than willing to assist me.

The following Saturday, I had an appointment to meet Jemal at his place to view the room and the apartment and J.P. was available to give me a ride. The apartment was in the Petworth area of D.C., about a mile and half away from Howard, going towards Silver Spring. The houses were bigger than the ones located directly next to Howard. We'd made a right on New Hampshire avenue and came around a circle, then got back on New Hampshire avenue. Drove down several yards, and there were some apartments on the right where we parked and I could see the address and it happened to be the one I had written down on a piece of paper.

We both got out the car and across the street, there was a Wachovia, Laundromat, liquor store, grocery store and dry cleaners right across the street from the apartment building and there was a bus stop directly in front. This was already feeling like it would be a great place to live. We went up to the building and pressed the button to get into see apt# 307. Jemal let us in the door immediately. We walked into the living room/dining room which was really spacious. There was a step down and an armrest leading us down into the area. You could see the kitchen as soon as you walked in and there was an inlet with no door, which showcased an all-white refrigerator, dishwasher and stove, all surrounded by light oak cabinetry. I could tell that Jemal had cleaned up because there was not a dish or dash of dust in sight, and everything seemed to be packed away nicely.

"Dontae I am so glad that I met you, I have been ranting and raving all week to my friends and classmates that I think I found the perfect roommate!" Jemal confessed.

"Well the place so far looks right up my alley and it's in a convenient part of the city. Plus all the added amenities with the bus stop being right out front and the strip mall across the street with the grocery store, liquor store and bank," I replied.

"Yeah that is one of the reasons I moved to these apartments. Let me show you your room and bathroom. I did tell you that you will have your own bathroom, because I have one connected to my bedroom. I never use the one in the hallway right here," Jemal said, turning on the light.

"My own restroom is definitely a bonus I never had my own bathroom before. I am used to sharing and when I lived in the dorms and was running late I hated having to wait for someone to get out before I could get in, because it made me even more late." I laughed.

"Well, all the reason to upgrade your standard of living. And trust me, the rent is real dirt cheap for northwest. Since I have been here for a while my rent is stabilized and hasn't changed since I moved in. But if you were just moving in then you would have to pay almost $250 more per apartment. I am really not trying to move because the only comparison rate would be in a neighborhood that is a lot sketchier than what I am already in. I want to stay put."

"Yeah I most certainly understand your concerns and I like the apartment so far, and I guess this would be my bedroom?" It was located directly across the hallway from the bathroom. There was enough space for a full- or queen-sized bed, with enough space for one or two more dressers. With enough room left over for me to walk around I thought. Jemal showed us his room as well; it was a little bigger than mine. He had a queen-sized bed in his room, everything was immaculate and in place. I could tell that he spent most of his time in his bedroom because he had a television, computer, stereo and Playstation. He had it color-coordinated with a cheetah print comforter and everything was either black or brown, with African Art and pictures hanging around the room. It looked really cozy.

There was a calendar of all men that was hung up in his personal bathroom. I was sure J.P. saw the calendar. I was almost certain that if she didn't know before, she knew now that Jemal was gay. I was sure that made me gay in her eyes as well. Gay by association! I could really see why a lot of straight men did not hang around openly gay men, because women automatically assumed their preference. I didn't have a problem letting J.P. know the deal with me, but I did hope that we remained friends because I really liked her a lot.

After I saw every nook and cranny of the apartment I was content that this could be my new home. I could tell however that Jemal had somewhat of a crush on me. He'd been trying to get me to go to dinner with him all week. I had been so busy with schoolwork and I really didn't want to mix business with pleasure so I didn't take him up on his offer. This was the only reservation I had moving in with him because I really didn't want there to be a potential problem. Even though Jemal was really handsome, and successful, I wasn't really looking to get involved with anyone at the moment. School was enough, plus I wanted to get a part-time job so I could have some extra money to buy a car and some new clothes.

Even though I had brought all the nicest clothes that I had with me to D.C., my wardrobe was still lacking compared to most of the people that I had seen on my campus or riding the metro. In Seattle, what I had in my closet was always a step above everyone else. Seattle was known for "grunge" so even if you had money to buy the most expensive clothing you tended to dress down in Seattle. I never got accustomed to this fad that was permeating my city. Looking my best was always something that I took pride in. I felt like even if I'd woke up on the wrong side of the bed or was having a bad day that nobody would know it. I'd always put on a "happy face" and that meant dressing nice.

However, D.C. was a bit of a challenge with the kind of budget I was on. These folks dressed to kill and my homegirl J.P. fit right in. Don't get me wrong, my clothes weren't outdated or anything. I could get away with wearing something two or three times in a month in Seattle. But not here! You would think these folks lived in the mall. I was glad to be here though, I just needed to get my gear correct and find a comfortable place to call home.

After I was done looking at the place I told Jemal that if he wouldn't mind then I would like to be his new roommate. Of course he shook my hand real quick and told me that I had made a good decision. I could move in as soon as next Saturday and we could meet up during the week and he would give me the keys. All I needed to pay was my share of the rent and pay on time every month and I would be good to go. I knew I could do this. I wasn't overextending myself financially and I knew I would be able to get a car soon because the rent was a lot less than I intended on paying.

When I got back out to J.P.'s truck, I could tell that she had something on her mind. It was silent for about two minutes before I decided to break the ice and tell her that I was gay. I knew she saw the all-male poster hanging on Jemal's bathroom. As I said before we were guilty by association, so I just bit the bullet and was honest with my new friend. I just hoped she was going to be as opened minded as I hoped she'd be. "Well, thank you again for taking me to see the place. You have been nothing but hospitable ever since I met you. I am so glad we both arrived at the school together early." I said.

"You're welcome Dontae, I believe that God puts people together for a reason. I know that He has blessed my life and I don't mind being a blessing to someone else's life if the situation presents itself."

"Yeah, you do have a lot to be thankful for and I am so glad that you aren't the stuck-up and spoiled type. Anyway, so since we are becoming close, I wanted to share something with you that you may already know. I have a real hard time with this because I hate being judged and we don't live in a perfect world. But anyway, I am gay, and I am attracted to men, not women."

"Oh sweetie, I am not going to lie and say I didn't have my suspicions, but living in Atlanta I have picked up when guys could possibly be on the other team. Don't get me wrong it is not because you 'act' or look gay (whatever that means) but most men who spend this much time with me would be trying to get down my pants and you have yet to make a pass at me."

I laughed when she said that. "Well, yeah, I guess you are right, because you are one hot sexy lady."

"Yeah but not hot and sexy enough to turn you straight, am I?" By this point we were both laughing hysterically. I was assured that our friendship would continue on the great path that it was on since we met. Trust me, I wished her last comment was true, because it would be a blessing to have someone like J.P. to call my girlfriend, fiancé and wife. But I knew being true to who I was as a person and what I need inside to be fulfilled, no women could ever reach that inner core. I didn't even know the right man at this point. I did know that a man had been the only one to even get close to that core. This was why I believed homosexuality was not a choice. We were born with these feelings. It would be so much easier to fall in love with J.P., have a few kids, buy a house, go on trips, get our children through college, babysit grandchildren and die old together. Again that wasn't the life for me. I just hoped that I could find a life partner, who shared the same values and beliefs, was as hard-working as I was and who wanted to be with me forever. I wondered if this person even existed or would I die an old accomplished man, around friends and family?

After we saw the apartment, J.P. dropped me off where I was staying. When I walked into the basement apartment and saw how small it was, I was excited to be moving to my own spot and sleeping in my own bed instead of on someone else's couch. Don't get me wrong, I was grateful for the hospitality, but I could never live like this permanently. Tee and Felicia were gone when we arrived, so I decided I would get some studying done since there was some peace and quiet in the apartment. I decided that I would study my tort law. This seemed to be more interesting to me than any other subject I was taking at the moment. The law, as it was applied, provided for reimbursement or damages for wrongdoings caused intentionally or by negligence in civil suits. What law school tried to do was make you think about laws in many different ways through reading a bunch of cases that had already been tried and had judgments made. At the moment I was reading a case on tort law where a famous entertainer sued a newspaper for defamation of character for reporting that she was arrested and convicted for driving under the influence of alcohol.

Apparently the news was leaked to a newspaper from an intern whose boyfriend was on duty that night. The information was wrong and the entertainer was not being arrested for a DUI. She was being stopped because the car she was driving matched the description of a car that was used in a bank robbery. However, since the entertainer was in a rush to an important engagement, got upset and acted rudely to the cop, the officer decided to be an asshole and illegally searched the vehicle. He left the innocent entertainer handcuffed in a police vehicle for almost an hour. Anyway, at the end of the court proceedings the judge ruled in favor of the plaintiff, because the newspaper owed the plaintiff a "duty of care" when reporting the story. It would've required them to check the facts accurately and only report what was true.

I was really fascinated with everything that I was learning. I felt like I could use the law to be a more informed person. It also allowed me to know my rights as a U.S. citizen. I would not be the one to get taken advantage of by our legal system. I intended to apply myself and learn every bit of these laws that were being taught to me and have the laws embedded in the back of my brain for whatever situation arose.

I studied for about two hours before Felicia and this guy she was dating, Brian, came into the apartment. She said that they were on their way to see the new Harry Potter movie and asked me if I wanted to join them. I was sure she was just being nice, because she saw that I was sitting here alone. I'd said no for two reasons: first, I was not into the whole Harry Potter thing, and two, I was not trying to be a third wheel with her and her man. I politely declined and said that I had a lot more studying that I needed to do before the weekend was over. She said she understood and they were in the house for less then thirty minutes before they headed back out to their movie.

I went back to studying for another two hours before Tee came in. She came in at a good time because at this point my head was hurting from information overload. She said she had rented two movies, one scary and one drama. She was tired of men for now and just wanted to spend her Saturday sitting in front of the TV with popcorn and ice cream watching flicks. She asked if I wanted to join her, but I was getting kind of hungry and I wanted to venture out on my own to see what I could get into. Although "Two Can Play that Game" and "Candyman 2" sounded entertaining, but I didn't want to spend my Saturday in front of the tube. Plus I felt like I had been in the house for too long and I was feeling a little cramped and I needed some fresh air.

So I decided to take a shower, and put on some casual clothes and catch the metro to Dupont Circle, which was the gay part of the city. Felicia and Tee lived near the Howard/Shaw metro stop so I needed to get on the green line from that metro station and transfer to the red line at gallery place, which would take me to Dupont Circle. I didn't know how to get there at first but when I arrived to the metro station, I luckily saw a directory which listed all the stops and everything was color-coded. I was thankful for this, because the area I was in was a predominately black area and I didn't want to be embarrassed by having to ask a stranger or even the metro attendant how to get to the gay part of the city. Blacks can be so homophobic and I didn't want to have to deal with that drama. I wanted to venture out alone and enjoy the new city, which was my new home, for now.

I paid my money to get on the train, and I was shocked how clean and maintained the Metro was. This was my first time catching the Metro since J.P. picked me up for school every day. Usually when I was watching movies and saw the subway in New York City, it was usually crowded, with a lot of trash and debris. There was signs everywhere on the Metro in D.C. saying, "no food or drink," and "remember to take your belongings with you when you depart the train." When I boarded the train, there were even police officers patrolling the cars to make sure that no funny business was going on. This made me feel safe. I had never ridden on a subway before, so I didn't really know what to expect. The closest thing that they had to a subway in Seattle was the monorail, which was more of a tourist attraction. It took you from the Westlake Mall in downtown Seattle to the Seattle Center, where the Space Needle was. It was built in the sixties when Seattle hosted the World's fair, now called "Expo." I knew Seattle did plan on installing some sort of subway system in the near future; at least, that was what people had been talking about when I left.

When I finally arrived at Gallery Place, which was also Chinatown, the next train going in the direction of Dupont Circle was in three minutes the marquee said. I thought that was cool, that Metro was sophisticated enough that they would let you know when the next train was arriving. There were a lot of people waiting for the next train at this location. I could tell instantly the ones that were going to Dupont Circle. You had your young teenagers, talking loud and being flamboyant. They probably just came out and were heading to the area where they could be free and have some fun with people like them. Then you had your guys who didn't really appear gay from the outside, but you knew they were because they were "cruising" each other. What I meant by cruising was that they were trying to get the attention of others that they found attractive by walking past each other more then they should. They were giving too much eye contact, in hopes that they would catch someone's attention and they would give them the okay to come and talk to them.

When the train finally came I noticed a tall skinny black guy who was "cruising me." He wasn't really my type so I didn't really acknowledge his subtle advances. When I walked on the train he sat in the seat directly in front of mine and positioned his back towards the window so he could check me out from the corner of his eye. I wasn't really interested so I kept my eyes on the advertisements toward the ceiling for everything from evening classes to HIV treatment.

When I arrived to my destination there were two exits to get out of the Metro. I wasn't sure where I wanted to go so I followed the teenagers to where they were going assuming they would put me right in the thick of things. As soon as I got out of the Metro I realized how hungry I was and I needed to find something to eat fast. My stomach was talking to me. I didn't really want to spend the time ordering at a restaurant and waiting for the food to be prepared. As I was walking I ran into a Subway and a Burger King and decided I would eat something quick, so I could walk around and see what Dupont Circle was all about.

When I walked into the fast food joint, there were three guys sitting and eating to my left. The shorter brown-skinned guy got my attention first because he yelled, "Damn, Red, you sexy as shit," looking directly into my eyes. All I could do was ignore the comment and walk to the end of the sandwich line to place my order. He caught me completely off guard, and they were not the only ones in the restaurant. When I looked up all eyes were on me, so I was embarrassed to the nth degree. "I never seen you around here before, I know you can hear me sexy. What are you, one of those deaf boys that go to Gallaudet University or something?"

"You are such an obnoxious queen sometimes. We can't take you nowhere with us, without you bothering someone or causing a scene," said a taller guy that was sitting at the same table as the short brown-skinned boy who just put me on the spot.

"Yeah, Twan, you need to leave the man alone, he don't want you. Sorry for my friend's behavior. We just left the Fireplace down the street. We was getting our drink on and this one right here has let the liquor get to his head," the third guy at the table yelled at me, looking embarrassed. He was actually really attractive. He was about 5'5, with a creamy dark complexion, thick eyebrows, black short hair with waves that went from the nape of his neck to the top of his head. You could tell he spent hours with a do-rag on his head and carried a brush in his back pocket, the way his waves were situated so fine on his head.

I decided that I was going to say something and not be a mute. "It is all good; you guys continue having a good time, and thanks for the compliment Twan."

"You're welcome! We are on our way back down to the Fireplace. You should join us after you eat your food."

"There you go again. How you know he don't have plans? What makes you think he wants to come with us?" The taller one said.

"Thank you for the offer. What is the Fireplace anyway? I am new here and I just stepped out to get a bite to eat," I replied.

"It's just a bar – nothing spectacular, but it's really the only thing that is going on right now on a Saturday for us." By saying "us" Twan assumed that I was gay like he was, but he was right. Let me find out I got called out, I thought to myself and laughed. "Around midnight we are headed over to the Bachelor's Mill in southeast," he finished.

"Sounds like the three of you have your night all mapped out."

"Yeah we do. This is our usual Saturday night routine unless there is a party or we are out of town somewhere. " Twan replied. "Well, I will see you later hopefully."

So the trio left, and I finished ordering my food and sat down and ate it all. It really hit the spot. I ordered a foot-long tuna on wheat bread, with mayo, lettuce and tomatoes, with a bag of barbecue chips, and lemonade. I ate the whole thing. I was feeling good after I left. I was in a new city so I was like what the hell why not go to the Fireplace and see what's going on. I was feeling very adventurous so I walked down the street and the place wasn't hard to find. You couldn't miss it. There it was at the end of the block on the corner with a real fireplace displayed right out in front. I went right on in, like I'd been there before.

There were more white men than black men sitting around a square bar with TVs hanging from the ceiling playing house music videos. The video that was playing when I walked in was Whitney Houston's "It's Not Right but It's Okay." There was little light in the bar, but if you had great eyesight you could see what everyone looked like from across the bar. The bathroom was at the far end of the bar on the same side that you walk in. When I walked in the bouncer checked my ID and to my surprise there was no cover charge. I immediately went to the bathroom to check and see that I didn't have food in my teeth, and make sure I was looking like I was when I left the house. It was kind of tight in the bathroom and everyone who walked past when I was in the mirror bumped my ass. I didn't let the groping bother me.

When I went to the bar, I ordered myself a vodka and cranberry and stood near the windows on the other side of the bar. As I was sitting there I saw several people walk past me and head further down a hall that I didn't see when I first got in the place. Most of the black folks that I did see enter the joint walked right around and down the hall. So, of course I was curious to see what was down this hall.

I found another hallway down the hall and at the end of this hallway on the right was a staircase. This staircase led you to another bar that replicated the one downstairs in a square, but the entrance was on the opposite side of the bar. To my surprise, they were playing R&B and hip-hop, and mostly everyone who was up here was black, including the DJ. I saw the trio I met at Subway at the other end in a conversation with another group of guys. I really didn't know what direction to go in, and I was a little intimidated because when I walked in I felt like all eyes were on me. Ordinarily this wouldn't be a bad thing but I wasn't really prepared for the atmosphere. I had never been to a club and saw this many black men who were gay and I didn't know where to start. You had your tall, thin, slim, fat, muscular, black, brown, light brown. Hazel eyes, brown eyes, gray eyes and the different types of men go on and on.

I was so glad my drink was gone because it gave me somewhere to go and not just stand around. So I ordered another vodka and cranberry and the white bartender who looked to be in his fifties, with salt and pepper hair, was grinning all in my face. I didn't know if it was because he wanted a tip or he was feeling me? I went on ahead and paid my tab and left a dollar on the bar. I didn't know if he knew it was from me or not because it was so packed and he was onto the next drink as soon as he handed me my change. I turned around to a 5'8, dark chocolate brown skin man who was standing directly behind me when I turned around. He was very handsome and very well put together. You could tell he took time picking out his outfit. Everything matched impeccably and his skin was so beautiful and chocolate, with wavy thick charcoal-black hair. "This brother looks great," was all I could think to myself. He smelled like he was wearing expensive cologne, and his breath was like the air in a freezer—cool and fresh. He smiled at me with his perfect pearly whites and said, "Where you going? Don't I know you?"

"I am not sure, I can't say where I would remember seeing you at, but it is really nice to meet you. My name is Dontae," I replied and gave him a handshake.

"I am Darrel, I go to law school at Howard and my roommate is a 1-L at Georgetown like you. We met at the library one evening last week, it was very brief. We really didn't say much to each other."

"Okay, well I do go to Georgetown, so you do have the right person. How do you like going to Howard for law school?"

"Oh it's great, this is my second year and I graduated from the University of Pennsylvania. Administratively it was a lot to get used to because Howard is not on point when it comes to that, but everything else is great so it makes it worth it. Plus, I always wanted to have the black college experience. I am sure law school isn't nothing like undergrad, especially since the campus is so far away from the main campus, but it still majority black and that is what makes it so interesting and impressive."

"That sounds cool. So what brings you out tonight?'

"Just wanted to get out the house, I been studying all day so I decided to meet up with some friends for a few drinks then head over to the Mill for a drink. What about you?"

"Well I was really trying to get something to eat which I did before I got here, and some guys that I met told me about this spot. So before I head back in I thought I would check it out. I have been studying most of the day myself, so my brain was kind of fried."

"I feel you on that. It's really nice to finally actually meet you one-on-one. I was kind of hoping that I had the opportunity. Your accent is a little different – you must not be from the east coast?"

"Yeah, you're right. I just moved here from Washington State, Seattle to be exact."

"Well I have never been to Seattle, but I hear it is a nice place to visit. I have an aunt who moved there because her husband took a job out there. She really loves it."

"Yeah it's a nice place to grow up, I must admit, but I am glad to be on this side of the country. It seems like there is a lot more going on out here than there is in Seattle."

"Well you maybe right about that. So did you leave anyone back home waiting for you to come back? A fine educated brother like you must have someone wishing that you never left."

"To be honest with you there is this guy that I met right before I graduated, and we got close. He is in the military and getting out soon, but it isn't that serious. He and I were really just hanging out. I was teaching over the summer to save money to move to D.C., and I really didn't have much going on. We would go out to the movies, rent movies, go to clubs and just hang out. It was fun. I kind of miss him, but like I said, we just met. It is really too soon to catch feelings. I do however keep in contact with him, but I am sure that since I am not there, he is doing his thing and now I am bogged down with school."

"Well, I know if I were him I would have tried to convince you to stay or would be asking to be discharged so I could move here with you. How did he let something so good like you walk out of his life? I never understand some dudes."

"Wow, thank you for the compliment. I don't really consider myself to be all-of-that, so I never even thought of the possibility of him moving for me. I mean since we just met I thought it would be crazy talk. But we did spend my last day together in Seattle. He drove me to the airport and we kissed and left it at that."

"Okay enough talk about the past and you kissing anybody but me. I am getting a little jealous now. It seems like there are feelings that have not been expressed. I hope that maybe you and I can spend sometime together, watching movies and going out to eat. I am sure our schedules are pretty much compatible with the tons and tons of work that is required from being in law school."

He was a really attractive guy and very easy to talk to. Kind of short but his personality and everything else about him made up for that. He was very charming. I said, "That would be fine with me."

"Well we have been talking for a few minutes now and I see that your drink is almost gone. Let me refill it while I refill mine. What are you drinking?"

"Vodka and cranberry," I replied. I waited a couple of minutes alone while he got both of us fresh drinks. When he came back, I asked him where he was from. He said he was a military brat, but had spent most of his time on the Eastern Shore, before moving to Philly for undergrad. He said he had a little brother that played basketball for a community college, and a little sister who was still in high school. He was the oldest of three. He also said he wanted to become a lawyer because he wanted to make a lot of money. He'd spent last summer in New York working in corporate law for a top law firm. He said the pay was great but the work was long and boring and he barely got a chance to enjoy New York City.

I asked him about D.C. and how he liked it and was he seeing anyone special or met anyone since he'd been here? He said his first year in D.C. he had met a few guys on the Internet that just wanted sex and he hadn't met anyone serious enough to mention, but was hoping that would change with me.

I enjoyed the constant flirting. He was definitely someone that I didn't mind getting to know. I wasn't sure if I really wanted to get serious with anybody, but then I thought "what the hell was I thinking about getting serious for?" I just met the dude I needed to relax and just enjoy the moment. The fact that he was in law school made it an added bonus. We had something in common. When he asked me why law school, I decided to give him the textbook answer instead of ruining the moment with the sad details of my youth. So I said I always wanted to know the law, and be able to apply it to change people's lives that couldn't afford or have the opportunity to seek the adequate legal counsel for their issues. Which wasn't really a lie, but it wasn't the only reason for wanting to become a lawyer.

I bought he and I another drink after we both finished the drinks he had got for us. We continued our conversation until his friends came up and asked him if he was ready to head over to the Mill. I was kind of sad because I was enjoying the conversation, but it was getting late and I had planned to attend church in the morning with Felicia. I needed to wrap this up anyway. After his friend walked away Darrel asked me if I wanted to go with them to the Mill. I declined the invitation and told him that I really needed to get up early tomorrow and I didn't plan on being out as late as I was now. He said he was disappointed, but said that he would drop me off at Felicia's and meet up with his friends later since I told him during conversation that I took the Metro to Dupont Circle.

I took him up on his offer for the ride home, not because I didn't want to ride the Metro home, but because I wanted to finish spending time with him. He was really somebody that I could see myself talking to on a regular basis. We finished our drinks and walked outside to his car. When we got to Felicia's place, which took us less than ten minutes he was really trying to convince me to spend more time and enjoy the night. I stuck to my guns. When I was getting ready to get out the car he was like, "What, I don't get a kiss goodnight?"

Although I was attracted to him and could see myself doing more than kissing him. I didn't want to move too fast. I got out the car and said, "We have more then enough time to do all that and more."

CHAPTER 5

J.P.

My two months in D.C. had been a rollercoaster ride, from starting law school and trying to keep up with the reading and the assignments, to joining a band, from the rekindling of my friendship with Kenya, and to my new friendship with Dontae. I honestly didn't know how everything was going so great for me. I'd literally lost fifteen pounds because I couldn't find the time to eat!

I really didn't like eating fast food everyday, which seemed to be the only thing that was open when I was on my way home. After I'd practiced into the morning hours with the band and finished studying.

Kenya and I had been spending a lot of time on the phone catching up and talking about old times. There would be times when she called and I knew I needed to be studying or learning a new song or arrangement. I felt like I had to be there for my girl. I could tell she was an utter mess and lonely while she had been in D.C. I also noticed that she had done a 360 when it came to dating. I didn't mean to be rude, but my girl had turned into a little bit of ho. I keep hearing stories about this guy and that guy, all the jewelry and presents that she had been getting. She also had been telling me the details about the sex. The few times I had been out with her there were always a few guys she had slept with, and after she introduced me she was like remind me to tell you about so-and-so.

I was kind of getting worried about her too, because there was a lot of things she could catch. With black women having the highest rate of new HIV infections she really needed to be careful. Especially in this area where you couldn't spot a D-L man from a mile away, like you could in Atlanta. These men in D.C. could fool you like there was no tomorrow. They were fine, educated and more masculine than Rocky Balboa or Tupac. In Atlanta, you could tell the men who were trying to front like they didn't like dick in their butts or mouths. But here you had to watch out before you got tricked. I knew my girl was smart and always wrapped it up, but still you never knew what could happen in the heat of passion, and that condom slides off or better yet pops because he was hitting those walls too hard. Anyway I was praying for Kenya. I didn't want to lose her again. The past several months had been hard without her. She meant way too much to me to let anything get in the way of our friendship again. There was so much about her that I admired.

Kenya was athletic growing up and I was never the athletic type. She was the one that got me into going to the gym and working out. She played volleyball all four years in high school and was captain of the team in her Junior and Senior year. She won a scholarship to play at Boston University where her high school coach played in college but declined to go to Spelman. She was a high achiever, just like me, which was another thing that we had in common. Sometimes I felt as though I was looking in the mirror because she reminded me so much of myself. She was even president of her junior and senior year class, and graduated from high school with a 4.0 grade point average.

IT WAS FRIDAY AND I just woke up, started a pot of coffee and started listening to some rehearsal tapes of me and the band. I still couldn't actually believe that I was singing again. It felt wonderful. Every time I finished a song with my new group I had to pinch myself to know that this was real, and not one of the dreams I used to have soon after my mother passed.

I was so lucky to find this band too. I was looking through the Washington City Paper to see if any local bands or choirs were looking for singers and I just lucked out on this ad. It read: "Recently lost our lead singer we are looking for a soulful female who has a great voice." That was all the ad said and it had a number to call if there was anyone interested. I'd read the ad over and over for about ten minutes before I made the call. The guy who answered the phone had an accent that let me know as soon as he started talking that he was a D.C. native. The vernacular down here was very distinctive. He introduced himself as Ronnie, and said that there was still an opening. He also mentioned that he started the band when he was in high school. All of the members had gone to the same school, which was Duke Ellington School of the Arts. This school was one of D.C.'s prestigious markers for kids who aspired to be artists. Most of the students who attended had the passion and drive for the arts and wanted to pursue this once they graduated from high school.

Ronnie then told me that the band had been established for about five years and their former lead singer, Tanya, moved to N.Y. after securing an understudy roll for one of the characters in the musical "Chicago." After hearing that, I was kind of overwhelmed because this Tanya must've been really talented. I knew right then if I was going to fill her shoes, I was going to have to wow Ronnie and his band. He asked if I had time to come check them out the same day that I called because they were rehearsing that night. I was kind of rusty in the singing department and I wanted to practice on my own before I showed off what I got from my momma. I made up an excuse about having to study, which wasn't a lie because I had a lot of reading that I needed to get through for my classes. I told him that I was in law school at Georgetown.

This seemed to kind of trigger a little hostility in his voice, and he was about to hang the phone up, but he said, "We are looking for someone who has singing in their heart. We want someone who can't live without singing. This isn't just a band that we do part-time. This is our passion. We are real artists with music in our bones, so if you're interested then I suggest you meet me tonight or maybe you should try out for another band."

I took a deep breath and thought to myself, "I know this guy was not dismissing me before he even got a chance had to meet me and hear me sing." But the way he felt about his band and music in general gave me inspiration and drive. I knew right then I was going to be the lead singer of his band and his passion was going to ignite a flame in my soul. I wrote down the address to where he lived, knocked out some reading and headed to my audition.

Ronnie's home was in the northeast Trinidad section of the city, which wasn't a very flattering part of the nation's capitol. If I didn't have the type of conversation that I had with him over the phone, I wouldn't have gotten out my truck. I would have turned right back around. When I got in the row house, I could tell this was a bachelor's pad – there was a large screen TV with a Playstation and Xbox in the living room. There were also weights and a basketball on the floor near the dining room. He had a real nice maple wood dining room table, but it had mail and papers all over it. I knew that no women lived in this place, and it was in dire need of some dusting and mopping. He led me to the basement where the band practiced. There was a keyboard, electric guitar and drum set. There were two mics on a stand and the keyboard and drum set with microphones connected to them so the band members could sing backup.

Even though I was on time everyone was sitting down in the basement in their respective spots as if they were anticipating my arrival, and this made me even more nervous.

Ronnie introduced me to Tay, who played the keyboard, and Ro, short for Roland, who played the drums. I could tell they were impressed by the way I looked because they couldn't keep their eyes off of me. I kind of felt like a piece of meat but I used this to my advantage and started to loosen up.

They said they wanted to warm up before I began my audition which didn't bother me. When they started playing the music it sounded very familiar to me, like I heard the songs before but they had a different kind of sound and style to them that made you want to dance and move around. I later found out it was "Go-Go" music.

Ronnie and the other band members explained to me that "Go-Go" originated in D.C. and it was the sound of the district. In order to get folks who have never listened to it before they do remakes of popular songs and tweak them with the "Go-Go" sound and sometimes the songs are even better remade this way. He also said that the most popular group that had crossover appeal was E.U. with "Da' Butt" which most likely everyone in America had heard. It was a timeless song because it could be played anywhere at any time and it was still played at birthday parties, family reunions, and anniversary parties and always drew large crowds to the dance floor.

I decided to sing "Have you Ever" by the popular singer Brandy, who became more popular after having her own television show. I closed my eyes and belted out the first verse and as I closed my eyes and they started playing their instruments behind me, I lost myself in the words, and started thinking about my mother…

As much as I loved her, she shut down after my father left and would never again open up to me and give her heart to me. I tried getting the best grades in school, always came home before dark, didn't do the dating thing that most of the girls in my high school were doing. I thought if I was the best daughter that a mother could have, then she would be the mother that she was when I was a tiny little girl. By the time I finished the song, I was in tears and everyone in the band was looking at me in awe.

Ronnie went to get me some tissue and when he came out he said that I could definitely sing. He said he wasn't a Brandy fan and didn't think she was that good of a singer, but I made him like this song. He said that I sung it better than the original version. His only criticism was that he felt the song was all about me, and if I wanted to sing for an audience I needed to open up and make it about the people that I was singing to. There was no reason for my eyes to be closed through the entire song. So he had me do the song over several times until he was satisfied that I was singing to them and not just to myself. This was really hard for me, especially with this song, because of all the emotion. Ronnie kept saying: let it out, open up to us, you can sing.

At the end of the night I learned two of their original songs that I really enjoyed singing, and was offered the lead singer of their band. Ever since I'd been going back from school to band practice to the library barely getting any shuteye or adequate nourishment for my body. Although I wasn't taking care of myself properly I was enjoying every minute of my new life.

The following day was my first public performance. We were opening up at a popular "Go-Go" club in D.C. for one of the hottest bands in the area. I invited Kenya and Dontae to come out and see us perform. Kenya didn't like this particular style of music since first hearing it when she moved to the area. However, she said since I joined the band she was going to support me, and I told her that she would probably end up liking it after going to a full concert and hearing us live.

We didn't have costumes or anything like that. Ronnie just said plan to look nice, since I would be the center of attention. I guess he didn't know me all that well, because that was something I didn't need to be told. If I was stepping out especially if I was going to be the center of attention, I was always going to be one of the flyest women in the room. That went without saying. Over the past month I'd taken a very deep liking to Ronnie. I knew the other band members could tell that we were flirting back and forth with each other since my first rehearsal. I was usually the last to leave, because he was always giving me tips on how I should breathe and elongate certain words when I was singing to make the performance sound better.

He was always grabbing me around my waist or putting his hand somewhere on my body to teach me the proper breathing methods. He learned that technique from his vocal coach when he was in school. Every time he touched me my body tingled, I got warm instantly and started to sweat lightly. I was sure he noticed my body temperature rising from normal room temperature to fever status, but he never reacted to my uneasiness – he was always so serious and focused on the band's sound. I knew I probably shouldn't had been having these feelings but I couldn't help myself when I was around him. He was so confident and sure of himself; he reminded me of my father, just more rugged and younger. During our last rehearsal, I just knew he was going to reach over and kiss me. He was standing directly in front of me. There was a space less than inches separating our bodies from each other. He had both my arms held to my side and we were going over a song that he had written for the band. He was trying to teach me the arrangement because I wasn't familiar with the song and he wanted me to repeat after him.

The song was about two people who were deeply in love but didn't know how to let the other one know. How ironic, I thought, when compared to our situation. He was looking directly in my eyes, asking me to repeat after him. When the band finished playing I could have sworn I saw his head move towards mine. I closed my eyes in anticipation for a kiss.

Five seconds later he was back at his microphone getting ready to pick up his electric guitar. I felt silly and made up an excuse and said I really needed to study for an exam that I had the next day and I was behind on the reading. Although this was the truth, I probably would have stayed longer and stayed up all night for my exam, but I left feeling humiliated.

I later told Dontae what happened. He said I shouldn't worry about it; if the chemistry is how I said it was, then sparks were bound to happen sooner or later. I just needed to be patient. He thought that Ronnie didn't want to cross the line because he didn't want to mess up the groove that was going on between the band and me. I agreed that he was probably right, but it still didn't fill the void I was missing from wanting him to take our friendship to another level. I was not the type of girl to throw myself on a guy. I would much rather him make the first move. This gave a girl a certain amount of control over the relationship to know that a guy went out of his way to show her that he really liked her. Maybe I was a bit old-fashioned, but I decided that would be the only way anything would ever exist between Ronnie and me, only if he'd made the first move.

After talking to Dontae, I bottled up all my feelings and emotions and went to Georgetown, the shopping district, to pick up a dynamite outfit to wear at the performance. I wouldn't see Ronnie again until the sound check at the club Saturday afternoon. We planned to go back to his house after that for lunch and practice until it was time to leave.

I told myself that I would just continue to be me and that I wasn't going to change just because I was falling for this man. I knew I could pull it off: hiding emotions and acting like everything was okay was my forte. If anyone knew how to mask her feelings, it was me. I could be the queen of fakeness.

When I got back from shopping, I still didn't know exactly what I was going to wear tomorrow. This was my first time going to Georgetown and I didn't know that there would be so many stores. I went on a shopping spree!

Since it was getting cold and I love boots. I bought two pairs of boots that looked very sexy on me, a black and a red pair, that go past my calves. I bought a few pairs of stockings because I knew I was going to be wearing a short skirt. I actually found a cute black one that was really short and would show off the boot and a little bit of thigh. I was so surprised because when I went to try it on in my size it didn't fit. I dropped one full size to a four and I liked the way I looked in this dress. I almost felt remotely conceited admiring myself in the mirror; standing up singing those songs had done some wonders to my legs. They were tight and muscular and I felt taller. I took the boots out and tried them on in the dressing room. I looked damn good. I just needed to find some tops so I could roll and get some studying done. I went to a few more places and picked up a few t-shirts and a blouse that I could wear tomorrow since I was still undecided.

When I got back to my apartment I headed to my bedroom turned on my reading light and started cracking some of the reading that I needed to get done. Believe it or not, school wasn't going as well as it could. I was now debating on why I went to law school, because I hated it. The only reason why I even went to law school was because after my mom died I didn't know what I wanted to do with my life. But after joining the band I knew singing was what I wanted to do. Singing was my passion and I needed to figure out what I wanted to do with myself before I ended up wasting an opportunity someone else could have had. I was taking up their place because I did well on my LSAT, and graduated with honors from undergrad. I was thinking after this semester I was going to drop out and start looking for a job so that I could start making money with the education that I had and dedicate more time to singing.

I knew I wasn't doing particularly well in school because I'd been spending most of my time singing and learning new songs. I knew I wasn't getting an F in any of my classes, but I was barely getting by – something that I wasn't used to doing. I knew I'd better finish while I was on top so if I wanted to come back I would be able to. So I continued my weekend studying until I fell asleep. I got woke up at quarter past ten to my father's call.

"Hey Baby, I must have woke you up because you sound terrible," he laughed.

"Yeah Daddy, I was knocked out. I had such a long day, law school is kicking my butt. I didn't know there was this much studying in the world," I replied. I wasn't about to tell daddy that I started singing again. I remembered when I was in high school he almost had me dropping out to join an all girl-group after he saw me perform at a school talent show. The group later became popular selling platinum albums which added to my father's riches and success. My mother advised me not to, said that I didn't want the fast life and that I should enjoy my youth while I had the chance. And as much as I wanted to and my father was pressuring me to, I decided to do what my mother advised. Once again I was trying to be the best little girl who would make her happy and maybe she would open up to me like she did when I was a little girl. When I later saw the girls perform at a club when I was going to school in Atlanta, I couldn't help but think that that could have been me on-stage performing and getting the crowd excited and motivated.

"Well, you have always been the studious type. I guess you must have gotten that from your mother because school and I was never a pair."

"Yeah I know, daddy, you tell me that every time I tell you that I have a big test or that I planned to study all weekend."

"Well I called to tell you that I will be in town tomorrow night and I thought that maybe you and I could go to dinner or something after I check out a few producers in the area that are becoming popular. I might use them for some of my acts."

Hearing what he said woke me up instantly. I didn't want my father to have anything to do with my music. I wanted to do this on my own. If the band that I was going to be in was going to make it we would have to catch the eye of some other record executive. I saw how my father controlled all his other clients. I didn't think we needed his guidance we would be able to make it on our own. "Oh really Daddy, well I wish you would've told me earlier I have plans tomorrow night that I can't break. Can we do brunch Sunday morning? What hotel are you in? I promise to be there to pick you up and take you to a nice brunch."

"That's fine baby, I will be staying at the Ritz Carlton downtown on 23rd street. Just call me before you come so I will be ready, and good luck with your studying. I love you and I'll see you in a couple days."

"Love you too daddy and I can't wait to see you," I said and put the phone on the receiver. My father had really made a conscious effort to be in my life since my mother died. I mean we always had summer trips and Christmas together. Now daddy made time to meet up with me at least once a month, sometimes twice. I really enjoyed our time together. There was nothing like it; getting to know my father in a way that I didn't know anyone else was amazing. I saw myself in his eyes the way he talked; I talked just like him. Growing up I was daddy's little girl but this was so much different, he wasn't just daddy anymore, he was a real person that made mistakes and was vulnerable. I'd never saw this side of him when I was younger.

I couldn't wait until tomorrow to perform live for the first time. I fell asleep and had a dream that a year from now I would be performing on a stage. I was in front of a large audience crying, and singing my heart out. I was content with my life: I had finally found what I needed to do in this world. So you know I woke up happy as a mug, and I decided to clean my apartment as soon as I got up and took a shower. Not the touch-up I'd been doing all week to make it appear that I had a little domestic home training. I knew the three clothes hampers that I had lined up inside my walk-in closet were overflowing and the bathtub needed scrubbing from me shaving my legs yesterday.

It was about ten o'clock when I finished folding the last towel and putting all my laundry away. I decided to go to the grocery store and stock up on a few things that I was missing. My place was back to being immaculate – you could almost eat off of every nook and cranny in the place. I washed two loads of laundry in my stacked washing machine and dryer in my bathroom. I cleaned out all the junk and leftovers that were in my refrigerator, swept, mopped and vacuumed every area of the house. I had been so busy lately I had left carry-out from several places; McDonalds, Burger King and Popeye's bags were left in the refrigerator. I cleaned everything out and my refrigerator was empty. Since I decided I was going to the grocery store I needed stock up on more than just food. My period was coming any day. I only had one more maxi-pad left in my purse. The coffee was getting low in this mug, and I needed some fabric softener.

When I pulled into the parking lot there were several cars in the parking lot that let me know I wouldn't be just running in and running out. This was a pet peeve that I hated about the grocery store. It always took longer then it should to get out of this place. As I walked in I scanned the front of the store and all the cashier lines were open. There were lines that were almost to the aisles. I made sure that I only grabbed fifteen items or less so I could go through express checkout. I spent about thirty minutes before I got to the register and started paying for my things. There was a short black full-figured young woman with really cute fat cheeks that worked the register. She had cornroll extensions that ended all the way down her back. The cornrolls where tied so tight and looked real fresh, you knew she was in pain while she was getting them done. I was sure she stayed up later than normal the night she had them put in. The pain may have even had her up all night. She'd probably woken up the next day tired. The things we black girls did for beauty I thought.

The one other thing that I noticed was this young guy bagging my groceries. He was medium-brown, perfect skin tone, really nice pronounced features. His eyes, nose and mouth were all pronounced and he had real thick eyebrows and sideburns that lead to a nice grade of twists on his head. This little boy was fine I thought as he bagged my groceries. When he was done and I paid the bill, he asked if I was going to need help outside. Even though I could carry my groceries myself I decided to take him up on his offer just because I could. I thought it would be harmless lusting after this fine young man. It wasn't like I planned on taking him back to my apartment. It had also been a long time since I had gotten some. I knew this boy was way too young to even mess with, but you don't go to jail for looking. I allowed him to take my groceries to my truck. When I got to my truck he told me his name was Ramone. I thought what a cute name for a cute boy his mother must've known he was going to be fine. "Well, nice to meet you Ramone," I said, purposefully not giving him my name on cue. "As you can see this is my truck, so you can go ahead and unload them in the back."

"No problem, no problem Miss," he said trying to be cool and manly. I guess he knew he was dealing with an older woman and he knew how to behave. I also saw him checking my booty out. After he loaded the groceries, I reached in my pocketbook and handed him a five-dollar bill. He said thank you and I walked to my truck to get in. When I pulled out the parking space I noticed him walk over to an older all-white Oldsmobile Cutlass Supreme in mint condition with pimped-out chrome rims. He opened up the trunk and got a bag out, and walked back to the front of the store. I was sure he had a line of young girls throwing their drawers on the back seat of that car. At least I knew the black race was here to stay, because these youngn's were killing it out here. I didn't remember seeing boys like him in my high school. He had the confidence of a man my age. I could see why these older women had been going to jail trying to get their groove back. He could probably make a lot of grown women feel like they were hot. "Lord, let me stop lusting after this young boy, please forgive me," I laughed to myself as I drove back to my place.

When I'd got back into the house I put all my groceries away and decided to do some much-needed studying while it was still early. I knew I didn't have to be at mic check for another several hours so I decided to go to Starbucks to study so I wouldn't be tempted to do something else. Plus I didn't want to spend a lot of time picking out my outfit to wear to my first gig. I always looked my best when I was rushing to get out the house. I didn't know what it was but my last-minute selections always got the best compliments. I knew I went shopping yesterday, but I still was unsure what I was going to wear exactly. Don't get me wrong, I always looked my best, but I was trying to look exceptional.

When I got to Starbucks I found a table in the corner where I didn't see anyone close to me so I could be distracted. I put my book bag down and ordered a Grande coffee and a rice-crispy treat which I loved. I sat back down, unloaded my torts book, took out my pack of high lighters and my notebook, and by the time I got everything ready for a rigorous study session the barista called my number and said that my order was ready. I went up to get it, sat back down and cracked the book open. I didn't look back up until two hours later when my cell phone started vibrating in my purse. My coffee and rice-crispy were completely gone. I looked to see who was calling me and it was Ronnie, so of course I picked up the phone real quick. Come to find out he was calling me to let me know that the headliner was running late and we needed to be at that the club in thirty minutes to do mic check. The headlining act was going to take our rehearsal slot.

The venue was on U-street and I had been there before to another club so I pretty much knew what direction I was going in. When I located the address to the club, I was excited because there was a metered spot right out front with just enough room for me to parallel-park my truck. I walked up to the front of the club, and I just remembered that I needed to be at Ronnie's place an hour before we were supposed to perform so car service could take us to the club. We would be ushered behind back to a dressing room where all of us would patronize so that we wouldn't mix with the crowd. I thought this was really special considering this was my first time performing. Since Ronnie was a D.C. native and he and his group were known around town they treated us like stars. This time I guessed since nobody was here I could walk up and go in like I was just me, J.P., but of course I had my stunner shades on just in case. Not really just in case because I was sure nobody recognized me yet, but I was sure Mariah and Patty would be all decked out in shades coming to a club for mic check. This was my dream so I had better act like one of them, because someday I hoped to be.

As I walked into the club the door was open and it led you into a vestibule where there was a curtain hiding the entrance into the club. I imagined when the club was in full effect that someone would be standing here checking ID and taking money for admission because of the register I saw along the side. I let myself through the curtain and I saw the rest of the band warming up on the stage that was situated at the back of the club. They were playing the first song that we were going to sing which was a "Go Go" remake of the famous song that was made popular by Brandy, "Have You Ever." This song meant a lot to me and I was very proud and honored to perform this song.

I went right up to the mic and started singing in the middle of the stage just like I did when I was in Ronnie's basement: running late from a study session, or a late afternoon being at Starbucks. However, this time was special and it invoked more feelings just to know that I would be onstage. I closed my eyes and thought about the situations in my life that portrayed the lyrics of the song. I knew when the audience was here that I needed to find a way to connect with them so they could picture their lives through me. This was something I knew I could do and what every natural-born singer was born to do: to touch the people that they were singing to. I needed to be sure that their hearts were being touched just as much as mine.

After the mic check, we completed two full sets of both songs that we were going to perform. The second was an original song written by Ronnie, which was more up-tempo to get the crowd rocking and into the music. It was the traditional "Go-Go" sound with all the instruments being played. The person setting up the bar along with the club owner was making sure everything looked nice in the club. To my excitement we had them rocking to the beat. After we finished the club owner whose name was Carlos came up to us and said that he was glad that he had booked us. He said the crowd was going to love us.

After we finished our mic check the other band that we were opening up for was just arriving. I saw what must've been their lead singer; she was the only female with the group at the bar ordering a cocktail. She was dressed in a sweat suit with Chanel sunglasses on her forehead looking real casual. I guessed she liked to get her drink on because she was drinking Hennessy straight up. My type of girl, I thought to myself. Even though a drink would have been relaxing, I knew I wanted my first performance to be clear and free of unnatural substances so I could take it all in.

We left without anymore introductions. The manager informed us that there were only two dressing rooms in the back that were reserved for the main act. He said there was a men's and women's restroom in the back for some last-minute touching and freshening up, so we needed to come ready to perform. I was kind of confused because Ronnie said that we had a dressing room, but I just went with the flow. I just said okay and got in my truck to roll out and get ready for the night. I checked my cell phone since I left it charged in the truck and I had one message from my daddy checking up on me, making sure that our plans were still on for tomorrow.

I found his number in my phone and pressed the button to call him back, "How is my favorite daughter in the whole wide world?"

"Be quiet daddy I am your only daughter unless you have some illegitimates out there that I don't know about," I replied.

"How is my intelligent daughter doing today? I know you are probably busy studying away becoming that bigshot lawyer you said you wanted to be?" Only if he knew I thought.

"My day is going pretty well, I went grocery shopping to pick up a few things for my place and of course I studied today. I am actually on my way back home. So enough about me and my day, how is your day?"

"Everything worked out well. I met up with some real good producers that I am thinking about using for my upcoming projects. The D.C. music industry is kind of up-and-coming, but there is a lot of talent down here. I see D.C. becoming the next Philly. There is very unique sound that comes out of this city that the world hasn't quite tapped into, and it's not just the 'Go-Go' I am talking about, but the song and the voice of the people of our nation's capital."

"I know what you mean daddy D.C. is like no other place. The people are from all sorts of places in the country and the world rather, and for the most part everyone is making money and doing things that black folks would only dream about doing. I am so glad that I am able to experience this."

"Yeah baby I am glad you are experiencing it too. I always loved coming down here in my younger years even thought about moving down here, but NYC is my home and I cannot imagine living anyplace else."

"Yeah I understand your love for NYC a lot of people feel the same way that moved on. NYC is the melting pot of the U.S., and has every nationality you could imagine. It is so unlike any other place I have ever been."

"Yeah you're right baby girl, but anyway I was just calling you to let you know that I am back at the hotel and I am meeting up with some old friends for some drinks out in Maryland later. I was just checking up on you."

"Thank you daddy for looking out, you have fun tonight and I will see you tomorrow." I hung up the phone after I heard him say I love you too and sat my cell phone on the passenger seat. I had all four bars, so there was no need in plugging it back up to the charger.

WHEN I FINALLY GOT BACK to my apartment I decided that I would take a bath, and soak my body since I had a few hours before I needed to be back at the club. I had this sensual bath bead set that I had gotten from a sorority sister for my birthday that felt really silky on my skin. I decided to pull out the kit after I turned on the water.

I got in the tub and closed my eyes. I dozed off for a few minutes and I remembered the dream that I was having. I was dreaming that after the show tonight Ronnie and I had went back to his place, and we made love. I woke up just before I was about to climax. My nipples were rock hard and my kitty cat was wet and dripping. And it wasn't because of the water. I could feel my natural juices pushing the water out. I wanted to jump back in the dream, but I couldn't so I concentrated on Ronnie's physique and broad shoulders. I pictured him naked as I stroked my pearl with my wash scrub imagining it was Ronnie's tongue tasting and licking it slow and seductive until I let out a scream and climaxed.

This was the first time I masturbated since I had been in D.C., so this was a very intense stress reliever. When I got out the shower and lathered my body with lotion I felt rejuvenated. I had just got my hair washed, cut and styled at the beginning of the week by Kenya's hair stylist and she hooked me up. The cut still looked fresh. I had been tying my hair down all week to make sure it stayed that way because I didn't want to have to wait until today to get my hair done by a new stylist and ended up not liking it. To my amazement and surprise I liked it a lot. Once I got my clothes on all I needed to do was turn on my curling iron, bump the ends and I was good to go.

I checked my voicemail once I got my robe on. Ronnie had called and said that he would be picking me up, because there wouldn't be that much parking by the time we got to the spot. The car service had just called him and said they would be running late, and wouldn't be able to get us to the club in time. Thank goodness my period didn't come today I thought, because today might be the day that Ronnie made his move. I really liked Ronnie a lot and it would be nice if he stayed the night. Just for wishful thinking I decided to make sure I put everything away in its place, so my house wouldn't be junky if he did decide to stay the night.

CHAPTER 6

Dontae

D.C. had turned out to be really fun, although I was busy as hell. I'd finally secured a job working for the Georgetown Law Review, doing research and fact-checking on numerous articles sent to the school each week. I had moved into my new place with Jemal, and since we were both in school and working we barely saw one another. We had our own bathrooms and I could hear him getting dressed in the morning. I generally ended up leaving before he did. By the time I would get in the house from studying, which had been close to midnight especially since I was now working. He was usually in his room asleep with the door shut.

I hadn't been spending that much time out of school with J.P. anymore. She'd been doing a lot of practicing with her band. I went to couple of their performances around the city and she was actually really good. I was surprised the first time I heard her sing. I didn't know the girl had pipes like that. I swear she could be the next Mariah Carey or somebody. She had a crush on one of the guys in her band.

His name was Ronnie. I was not sure how close they were because she didn't like talking about him after he finally made his move. But every time she brought his name up she would get all giddy and started blushing. I was kind of worried about her and school because she had skipped quite a few classes. I knew she had been putting more time into singing than she had law school. Even though we were starting to become real close, I didn't think it was my place to be all in her business asking her why she was slacking in her classes. I did, however, try to get her to come to the library and Starbucks to study on the regular basis. Most of the time she had declined because of band practice. I just hoped she was able to balance both because I didn't want to see her fail any of her classes.

The Thanksgiving holiday was tomorrow. It was crazy how time just flew past me without me even knowing. Next month was Christmas and the end of the semester. Kenya had invited me to her place for Thanksgiving dinner. She was having a few people over at her place and since I would be in town with nowhere to go, (Felicia went back to Seattle and Tee was going to her parents home in North Carolina, and J.P. and her farther planned a trip to Jamaica) she didn't want me sitting home alone on Thanksgiving. It would have been nice to go back to Seattle and have Thanksgiving with my family, even though it was dysfunctional. My grandmother and my mother's sisters could throw down. I wanted to save up and buy a car and since I planned to go home for Christmas; I couldn't really afford go home for Thanksgiving too. Around the holidays tickets could run you from D.C. to Seattle anywhere from three hundred to seven hundred dollars.

I didn't mind staying in D.C. over the holidays. Although I still had a lot of work to do, I planned on knocking everything out the day after Thanksgiving. I wanted to spend the rest of my free time with Darrel. We'd planned to drive up to Atlantic City on Saturday and stay the night at one of the hotels and come back on Sunday. I'd been seeing him every free moment I had since I met him. He was very easy to be around, not to mention very easy on the eyes. We hadn't taken our friendship to the next level as far as sex yet. We'd decided to take things real slow. The consensus was that sex too fast ended up ruining what could be. Therefore we wanted to make sure that we got to know each other on a personal level more in-depth. However, there were moments where we both had to catch ourselves from our sexual proclivities. We would be at his place or mine sitting and watching a movie kissing, holding each other real close wanting to do more, but our minds wouldn't let our bodies take over. One of us would always go to the bathroom and simmer down, and come back out as if nothing happened. We had been doing this on a regular basis now. Even though we spent a lot of time together, we never spent the night together. Atlantic City would be the first time.

I wasn't sure what the sleeping arrangement would be – two double beds or a king since he made the reservations. I was hoping that we would finally take it to the next level because I was really feeling Darrel a lot and I knew that I wanted to be with him sexually.

There was a little tension at first when Jemal met Darrel. He kind of gave him the cold shoulder one night when Jemal came home and we were in the living room on the couch laying on each other watching a movie. Darrel had sensed the tension and when Jemal went into his room, he asked me about it. I told him that I sensed he had a crush when we first met. I thought since we were roommates that it would turn into just business and hopefully a good friendship.

Darrel said that I was too naïve in thinking that and told me to watch out, because a lot of dudes had their own agenda and you never knew it until you were caught up in it. I kept this in the back of my mind. Things had been weird ever since I had been dating Darrel. Jemal was very cold to me and had started complaining about every little thing. He even had the nerve to complain about the cleanliness of my bathroom which he never used: but said since it was the public bathroom then it should always stay clean. He then started complaining about how I didn't buy drinks or food for the apartment, and since we were roommates we should probably go shopping together and buy things for the place. I thought this was kind of ridiculous because I was barely at home. Plus I didn't see why he wanted to share groceries. We were cool, but not best friends. I wanted a roommate where I could do me and not have to worry about anyone else. I felt kind of sorry for Jemal because after getting to know him I realized that he really didn't have that many friends. It made sense because his attitude was really bad. He was selfish and wanted folks to cater to him. I also felt like he could be jealous of his friends in a mean way.

He had this friend named Carmello who was a really nice guy and came to the house from time to time. We would all talk and shoot the shit. However, when Carmello would leave Jemal would always have something negative to say about him: like he needed to get a better job, or he was a ho. I felt if he thought so negatively about him why when I came home he was always at the house?

I had tried my best not to allow Jemal to bother me or get under my skin. I did have to tell him that I didn't think the whole grocery-shopping thing was a good idea. I explained that I ate out a lot. Even though he cooked and I would eat sometimes I just thought he was being nice by sharing. I didn't need to pay for him to cook my meals because half the time I would have already ate before I came home.

I was glad that he would be gone for a few days. It would give me some peace and quiet and I didn't have to deal with his attitude. I hoped he would get over any feelings he had for me and realize that I was helping him out by paying half the rent. He didn't have to move his punk ass to southeast. He needed to forget about all this nonsense of us being together, if those were his real feelings, because it wasn't going to happen.

Darrel was going to the Eastern Shore to spend Thanksgiving with his family. He would be back in D.C. on Saturday morning and we would leave for Atlantic City.

D.C. WAS VERY INTERESTING because I was sure there was no other place where I would find another gay black man who I had so much in common with. It was known for its large population of gay black men, but you had to see it to believe it. I never imagined it would be on this scale or that there would be so many men to choose from. I knew there were some black men in other cities including DC who didn't choose to live their life exclusively dating men due to life's gruesome ridicule of our unions. The thought still remained in my mind: that if I truly had the option of choosing to be straight or gay and being equally content, I would be straight. Life for me would be a lot less difficult.

I was sure I wasn't the only gay man who felt this way. Moreover, some did live in the closet, had wives and kids and messed around on the side. Some of us didn't mess around at all. They suppressed their natural sexual urges and lived among the straight society, wishing they could feel the caress or warmth of another man on their flesh. The desire for a man to have sexual relationships with another man — give up his penetrating power — and all the status that it gives a man in this world is scary to most men, even gay men. This is why you have men who have sex with other men who don't like to identify themselves as bottoms—they allow other men to penetrate them. The fact of the matter is, when two men come together to have sex someone is going to have to be the bottom. In my opinion, curiosity is such that, even if you are the one doing the penetrating for years, whether it is with women or men; seeing someone enjoy anal sex and getting gratification that you have never once had the opportunity of receiving will spark a curiosity. This will make the man who had never been penetrated before in my opinion want to feel that satisfaction for himself at least one time in his life. If he likes it then he would seek out this sexual experience again. I had watched a show on HBO once where wives strapped on dildos and penetrated their husbands to satisfy them. For some sex is just an act. Being dominated and vulnerable in a sexual and intimate way isn't just something that is innate to women.

It is unfortunate that most men can't admit these things. You even have women who say that they would never partake in anal sex but you also have women who have done it on more then one occasion and actually like it. The society that we live in is so conservative that when it comes to sex many people are afraid to try different things; out of fear of what it would make them look like to the other person instead of just enjoying the person they are with.

When I first started experimenting with sex it was with boys and girls, but for some reason the boys were the ones who really got me excited. At first all I wanted to do was hunch, rubbing penises and skin together, that felt so fulfilling to me. But as I got older the boys wanted to do more. The next thing I was asked to do was perform oral sex, and of course at the age of like twelve or thirteen I thought it was gross and I didn't want to do it. I ended up doing what the boys asked though because I wanted to get what I wanted out of the deal which was hunching. Then when I was about fourteen I was asked to get screwed and I really didn't want to do that, but of course I tried it and it was so painful that I couldn't even get the head all the way in before I had to stop. The experience was so traumatic that I stopped going over that particular boy's house again. I always wondered if what I was doing was natural, or were my friends and I just too fast for our own good? I never took any child psychology courses to find this out so I guess I will always wonder.

It wasn't until my junior year in college that I actually met a guy I liked. He was twenty-two at the time and I was nineteen. He was a lot more experienced than I was. I made the conscious decision to let him have anal sex with me. It hurt in the beginning, but I liked him so much and he was so gentle and passionate that he made my actual first experience not even feel so bad. The funny thing was he didn't believe me when I told him it was my first time because I enjoyed it so much. I kind of wished I had waited until I was a little older and mature though. But I had always let curiosity get the best of me. Anyway, we tried to date but with me being a full-time student and active on campus our schedules didn't allow that much time for us being together, so it dwindled down to nothing. I would say this was my first heartbreak, because I really liked this guy.

The coping mechanism I dealt with to get over this hurt was being promiscuous. I would go to the clubs every weekend just to meet guys. I thought it would be rather easy to just find another boyfriend. But what I ended up finding was a lot of sexual partners. It kind of gave me a little bit of a reputation in Seattle. I was really only into black men, although there was one white guy that I'd met at a gay skate party one time that I had to get with and I did. So it got to the point where I had dated and had sex with mostly all the openly gay or D-L black men in Seattle that I could get my hands on. When it was time to graduate I had to move to a different city because I had outgrown Seattle, literally and figuratively. I told myself that I wouldn't make the same mistakes twice, getting caught up with all those different kinds of men. I was off to a good start by meeting Darrel. He had been really steady lately and our encounters had revolved around more than just sex.

I WOKE UP THURSDAY MORNING and had some cereal. I didn't want to eat too much because I knew since it was Thanksgiving that I was going to eat really good at Kenya's place. I knew it wouldn't be anything like I was used to back home. Kenya assured me that the food that she and her friends were preparing was going to be some down-home cooking. I was a little skeptical. She had planned to pick me up around three o'clock which gave me some time to get all my studying done so I could enjoy the long weekend. I did, however, want to watch the Macy's Thanksgiving Day Parade, which I always did since I was a kid. As soon as it went off I turned off the TV and cracked open the books.

Before I could even notice the time, I was receiving a phone call from Kenya asking me if I was about ready. She was on her way to pick me up. When I hung up the phone, I looked at the time and it was damn near three in the afternoon. I was really engrossed in this case on employment law and how in some states the law was on the employers' side and workers could be let go for any reason whatsoever that I lost track of time. So I rushed in the bathroom to take a shower, get some jeans out that I had hanging up and put on a sweater because the November weather in D.C. was quite nippy. I was praying that it didn't snow so we could still drive up to Atlantic City Saturday morning. I was brushing my hair when my cell phone rang again, and Kenya said she was outside. I rushed to put my shoes and my P-coat on and rushed out the house.

Kenya was in her Lexus smiling. "I hope I am not too prompt for you? Since I was the host, I didn't want anybody waiting outside my apartment for me, when they arrived. You know how folks get when food is involved they will be breaking your damn door down just to get a taste."

"Oh, no you're fine, I kind of lost track of time because it was so quiet but I am ready to go. Thank you so much for inviting me over to your home for Thanksgiving dinner. I don't know what I would have done if you wouldn't have invited me," I replied.

"A fine brother like you, I am sure someone would have felt sorry for you and took you in, just to look at you," she kidded.

"I don't know about all of that, but I bought a pound cake from the store across the street that I hope is good."

"Oh, you didn't have to do that but thank you. I am sure my greedy friends will eat it up, and I have just the dish to serve it on so folks will think it's homemade." We both laughed and drove to her place. I had never been to Kenya's apartment before, but I had seen her on several occasions while I had been in D.C., since her and J.P. were really close. I knew I would feel comfortable.

She lived in Adams Morgan, in some really nice apartment called the Woodener. I could tell she paid an arm and a leg, because there was a secured entrance with a doorman out front letting in guests. Not to mention the lobby was really large with a sitting area with a piano and flat-screen television. We found parking on the street right near her apartment building and took the elevator to the eleventh floor, which was the top. Kenya had it going on, she had a penthouse apartment that overlooked the city. You could see the monument and the capital from her living room window. She had a patio that you could walk out and get a better view of the city. I thought to myself that she must do well at the temp agency she worked for to afford this apartment.

"Make yourself at home. You can hang your coat up in the closet in the hallway, let me take the pound cake and put it in the serving dish. I will give you a tour before everyone arrives. I told everyone to be here around 3:30 – 4:00, so hopefully my friends who are bringing the major dishes like the mac and cheese and greens will be here shortly so I can finish setting up the table in the dining room," Kenya said. I waited for her to do her thing then she came out of the kitchen and we walked around her apartment. She had a nice setup. She had a great big kitchen with a full-sized dining room adjacent to the kitchen with large windows looking out to the skyline. The living room was very cozy with a matching grey leather couch, love seat and rocking chair. There was a bathroom in the beginning of the hallway near the closet where my coat was. There was a room with a day bed, computer desk, computer, printer, large bookshelf and matching credenza. She said this was her little "office slash guest room," but not too many people stayed the night in the room so it was more her office than anything else. Then at the end of the hallway was the master bedroom. The door was closed and she asked me if I was allergic to cats because her friend Elaine who was coming was, so she had the door closed so the cat wouldn't run out while Elaine was here. I told her I would be fine, and she opened up the door to a large room with a canopy bed and Lay-Z-Boy chair that matched the color of her comforter. She had black and white art on the walls of beaches and sand that made the room look really tranquil and inviting. What was breathtaking was her balcony. She had a balcony in her bedroom that had the same view that the living room had. I was sure she had spent some romantic times in this room. After I surveyed her bedroom I complimented her on how lovely she had everything decorated. She said she painted all the walls herself and picked out most of the art at Eastern Market, which was a popular flea market in southeast.

As we were walking back to the living room we heard someone knocking on the door, so Kenya walked to open it and I went to go sit on the couch in the living room. I could hear Kenya greeting her first guests and telling them where they could hang their coats. She said she would take the food and get it ready to be served. It sounded like it was a couple and when they walked in the living room Kenya introduced me to Elaine and her friend David.

Elaine was Kenya's assistant at work. They had gotten real close over the last year and David is one of Elaine's friends from high school. They both are from New York City and have to work tomorrow, the day after Thanksgiving, so they decided not to go home. David was about my height, but a lot slimmer; he was about fifteen to twenty pounds lighter than me. He was on the verge of skinny but he had broad shoulders and had real good posture so his weight looked fine on him. I could tell the dude was gay, he had that twinkle in his eyes, and we hit it off instantly. He told me that he worked full-time and went to school full-time working on his bachelor's in communication at Morgan State in Baltimore. David was really easy-going and very funny, and as more people started to pile in that neither one of us knew we kind of stuck together just talking about D.C. and NYC and the different clubs.

As soon as everyone arrived it was about ten of us. We said grace and made our plates. Only six people could sit at the dining room table, so David and I decided to sit on the couch and watch TV and talk while everyone else was at the table eating. Kenya and Elaine ate in the kitchen discussing their business plans on opening up their very own temporary agency that catered to finding jobs for minorities in the area.

After everyone ate, Kenya and Elaine cleared the table and Kenya asked if anyone wanted to play spades. I asked David if he knew how to play and he said of course so we decided to be partners.

We ended up staying on the table for the rest of the night beating out all our opponents. Our last game was between Elaine and Kenya after everyone had left and they had cleaned up everything. The game was to five hundred. We only needed five books to win and they needed eight, and there was a lot of shit-talking going on, because the girls had got set and went a blind six. That put them back in the game so they were excited and wanted to win and beat our three-game winning streak. They could had easily gone to seven and tied us, but no – they were way too overconfident and wanted to go the straight eight for the win and kill.

"I'm sorry I am going to have to do this to you guys, but this is my house and I will be winning in my shit," Kenya yelled. I could tell she was kind of tipsy because she was slurring a little bit. "After we finish whipping your ass we should all go out and get a drink and go dancing somewhere. I know some of us have to work tomorrow, but it will be a slow day so we should be all good for work."

"Where you wanna go girl? That sounds like fun. You the boss or at least mine so if I am a little sluggish tomorrow then you will already know the deal," Elaine laughed.

"I was thinking we do the Mill, I went there last year on Thanksgiving night and had a blast and considering we have David and Dontae with us, they should enjoy themselves. I am sure Dontae has never been to the Mill before. I am sure you have David."

"Yeah I always go and I should be okay for work in the morning. My boss won't be there so I can slide in anytime I want. Well not any time but as long as I am there before ten a.m. I should be good," David let us all know.

Now everyone was looking at me, and I really didn't have anything to rush to my apartment for other than studying. I had plenty of time tomorrow to get all my homework done before my trip to Atlantic City. Darrel and I promised each other we wouldn't bring any study materials. On our first getaway together we were acting like we had no cares in the world other than spending time with each other, and I wanted to see how we were going to make this happen. I took too long thinking about Darrel, and how I needed to make sure I didn't get into any trouble, because David was hot – not really my dating type, but still kind of irresistible. He was so cool though that I doubted I would even go there – anyway. I was just going to go out and have a good time, Darrel was my man and David was just a guy that made me feel real comfortable. "I am cool too, there is nothing keeping me from having a good time with you guys."

After I said that everyone looked at me and we finished up the game. The girls won because we only got five and they got their full eight so they won by ten points and all I would hear for the rest of the night from Kenya was how she whipped my ass at her house in spades.

We all piled up in Elaine's car with David and me in the backseat and the girls in the front. It took about thirty minutes to get on that side of town. The way people talked about the Mill made me feel like it was legendary. The Mill was similar to a rite of passage to most black folks who identified with the gay community. I had to admit that it was a staple and even if it shut down tomorrow folks would still be talking about the Mill.

The Mill was fine, but the drinks were way too strong. It was like they wanted you fucked up, incapacitated and dead to the world if you had more than one drink at their establishment. The drinks just made no sense; most businesses were worried about over pouring and high liquor costs. But strong drinks were their trademark and they were not hurting for business. No matter who was in town or throwing a party they would be open and it would be a profitable night, which was why they probably never sold or moved with all the gentrification going on in the area.

We all danced the night away. There were a few people I saw that I wouldn't have minded getting a little frisky with. I held on to my conservative not-so-freaky behavior and I took my ass home. I knew that this *had* to be the weekend that Darrel and I finally took our friendship to the next level. I'd been way too long without sex. With me going out last night and all the boys who wanted to go home with me and I wanted to go with them as well, I needed this consummation in order to know that my waiting wasn't in vain.

When the night was over and Kenya dropped me off. I was so intoxicated I could barely remember getting into the house and laying down in the bed. It was like 3:30 a.m. when I got in the house. I drank so much I didn't wake up until Friday afternoon at twelve-thirty. I couldn't remember the last time I woke up that late. Usually on the weekends I was up by nine since I'd been in D.C. I haven't had any mornings like this since leaving Seattle, and to be honest I felt rather rested.

When I got out the shower and put on some boxers and a wifebeater. Since I didn't have anything to do today and I was home alone, I felt I could be a little free. I saw that I had two voicemail messages. The first one was from Darrel letting me know he was hoping that I had a great Thanksgiving and apologizing about not calling earlier. He was surprised I wasn't answering the phone. He had been calling since six a.m. to wake me up and now it was ten and he was finally leaving a message to see if I was okay.

"Ain't that cute, he is worried about me," I thought to myself when I hung up the phone. I had a total of ten missed calls, which let me know this dude was blowing me up. I had one more message left, and I decided to call my voicemail again to see if he had left me two messages, but to my surprise it was David. He said he made it to work and it was so slow, he thought any minute they would be getting a memo saying they could leave early. He didn't know if I had plans tonight but he wanted to know if I wanted to go to a house party around ten and then head to a club afterwards. I was so not expecting this, plus I was really trying to save money and I knew I needed to have money for this weekend in Atlantic City. I was thinking about telling him no at first, but then I started to think about it some more, and I figured I might as well. I had nothing else going on.

Since it was Black Friday I decided to go to Georgetown on the Metro to see what I could buy to wear to the club, and possibly some nice boxer-briefs for while I was in Atlantic City. I didn't want Darrel to get turned off by my old tighty-whities that I usually wore.

I found a really great selection of boxer-briefs from this store called H&M. They had every color print that you can think of, plus a wide array of special prints of underwear. I was in heaven. I hated to admit it but this was very "gay" of me, I loved some nice underwear on me and the guy I was dating. The kind of underwear you wear says everything about you. I liked to buy underwear for the types of moods I was in. Darrel better watch out because he wasn't going to be ready for what I was going to be walking around in, in the hotel room.

I had to walk about a mile when I got off the blue line at Foggy Bottom to get to Georgetown. I saw several buses pass me by that I could have gotten on, but since I had never been here before I decided to walk around and take a tour of the west end of downtown. The brick stores and apartments leading into Georgetown were kind of cookiecutter; they had the same shape and style just different color painted brick and different color shutters and window treatments.

Since I was on a budget saving to buy a car, I was looking for the bargains. I went to the sales section of every store I went to. Everyone must have been feeling the same way I was because in every store the sales sections were a wreck. Hardly anything was folded and some of the clothes were mixed in areas where they weren't supposed to be. That did not stop me from spending $250.00 on two outfits and some shoes. I really didn't want to spend that much money, but I had never been able to give up a good bargain, and most of the time I ended up spending more than I should've.

Since all I had was cereal before I left, I had worked up a bit of an appetite. I just realized that I had eaten out more then I ever had in my life since moving to D.C. I had spent so much on McDonalds you would think I had stock or owned my own franchise. I had been picking up weight too, which wasn't cute. I knew the fat gene ran in my family, meaning that after twenty-one everyone got big and out of shape. They didn't look like themselves anymore because they had extra rolls in places in their body where they shouldn't have them. The one that developed first was the one right under your chin. It either looked like you had a double chin or your neck had rolls. That was the weight I was trying to stay away from, but I needed to start going to the gym and eating more healthy. My body was getting out of control, and I needed to be sexy when I took my clothes off.

So when I got near the metro I ordered a chicken salad from a little deli to bring home and eat. The Metro was real crowded getting back to the apartment and instead of taking the bus I decided to walk home, which was about a mile from the Metro. It wasn't that bad but if you were in a rush you would be assed out. You had to know the bus schedule to get to where you needed to go on time or planned ahead. I needed a car because I was not a morning person and it was killing me waking up so damn early just to get to class. I was so glad that next year I could start taking classes that didn't start until ten a.m. for me. My core classes that started at 8:30 were killing me. I would barely make it to class on time and it was beginning to show because my professor stopped class every time I was late and said, "Mr. Erickson, I guess you were up studying and preparing for my class that missing the first five minutes you would be so caught up and knowledgeable that you would get an A in my class? And you could answer this question that I was just about to ask the class what they thought?" He would then grill me with the subject that the class was discussing. Thank goodness he was right because I was up late studying. I was a night owl and that was when my thinking cap came on. I was always able to answer his question. No matter how hard it was and I had gotten a 97 percent on my first two papers. I knew I would be getting an A out of this class, but on about my seventh tardiness professor Kisner asked me to stay after class.

"You're a smart kid," he said. "You will probably do really well in law school because I can tell you take the time out to learn the material. However, in the real world punctuality is everything, so you need to gain the discipline to wake up on time and get to the places where you need to be. It may seem insignificant to you now, but people are always watching you and sometimes they won't appreciate your attitude for whatever reason and hold your tardiness against you, because they can, and you will lose out on an opportunity that you may really want."

I really took note of what he said and made more of a conscious effort to get to class on time even though I was a lazy ass. Since I moved further uptown, J.P. no longer picked me up for class. She was always running late too because of band practice.

FRIDAY NIGHT ALL I COULD THINK ABOUT was the next day and my trip. I wasn't really too focused on the people I met at the party and the club. The night was a little routine, we went over David's friend's place, played cards, won again, then headed to another club called Jenny's which was in an Asian restaurant at the waterfront mall in southwest. The men here were a lot younger and finer than the men from the Mill, even the bouncers and the dudes taking the money were fine. By the time we got to the club I was quite drunk, too. I had two vodka and cranberries while playing cards, and right before we left we took two tequila shots. I was almost pissy and I was hoping nobody noticed. I was able to get through the night but only barely, but as soon as I got back home I headed straight to the bathroom so I could throw up. I drank way too much!

I woke up the next morning to my phone ringing, and it was Darrel letting me know that he was an hour away from D.C. "Baby, I didn't just wake you up, did I?"

I lied. "No, I have been up for some time, I just have a headache. That is why I sound terrible." I did have a splitting headache and my mouth was so dry. I needed to drink some water fast.

"Well, I just wanted to let you know I am on my way. Would you like me to pick you up some Advil or something for your headache?"

"No, I have some and I should be fine by the time you get here. Let me finish getting my things together and I will see you when you get here," I said and hung up the phone real fast. I darted out the bed, turned the shower on and threw the clothes I was going to wear on the middle of my bed. I took a quick shower, did my last minute packing of my toiletries and made a bowl of cereal. I heard knocking at the door just when I was washing the bowl out and putting it the dry rack.

I opened the door and Darrel playfully pushed me into the apartment and slammed the door behind him. We rubbed our bodies together while holding each other tight. He started kissing me, and we kissed for about a good whole minute. When he moved his mouth from mine by this time my male member was standing at attention, as we headed to my bedroom. I had just made my bed minutes before his arrival, but I just knew it was about to get messed up again. He threw me on the bed and I was lying on my back. He mounted me with his knees on both sides of my hips, unbuckled my belt, pulled my pants and underwear down, lowered his head and took my member into his mouth. He then slid up and down with his tongue massaging every vein and crevice pulsating from my shaft, giving me joy that I had been waiting weeks to receive. I was about to release when he pulled my pants all the way off, lifted my buttocks up and directly in his face with my legs dangling from his shoulder down his back, and started licking me up and down. At this point all I could think about was how good it felt. I was screaming like a bitch, "Don't stop." He eventually stopped and laid next to me in the bed.

"I hope you're ready for Atlantic City because I am. The tank is full so let's go." Darrel said after he abruptly stopped satisfying me.

I was in utter shock. How could he just tease me like that? We didn't even bust. But it only took me a second to recover. I didn't say a word. I just got my things locked up and headed to his car.

CHAPTER 7

J.P.

Now that the semester was over, I was so glad to be done with finals. I had barely passed. If it wasn't for Dontae and our power-study sessions I would've been toast. However, my boy came to my rescue and we knocked everything out cold. Of course I didn't get the same grades as Dontae, but I did pass and that was all that mattered. Now I could really focus on singing and maybe a career without having schoolwork to think about. I knew I was spending Christmas Eve and Christmas Day in NYC with my father and his wife, but I had a singing engagement over the break. We were scheduled to open up New Year's Eve for Backyard. Backyard was a popular "Go-Go" band in the area and was throwing a big party downtown at the Lafayette Center. It was a place where rich white people threw weddings and parties.

Over the past several months I had become a hit in the local establishments that feature "Go-Go." It was more of a D.C. thing and very local. The surrounding areas loved "Go-Go" too they picked it up from listening to D.C. radio stations and going to clubs. But I was really trying to get Ronnie and the group to play more music that was more mainstream, without all the instruments. I wanted us to have more of a crossover appeal so we could start performing at places that my friends liked to party. Places like Dream or the Avenue. I just figured that "Go-Go" would only get us so far, and people liked us already. And I thought more people would like us as well if we didn't pigeon hole ourselves in just performing "Go-Go."

Ronnie just didn't see it my way. He was comfortable in D.C., just with a large crowd. He didn't care as long as he had a crowd, but for me I felt like I wanted to touch the world and meet larger and different crowds. I wanted to go to London, South Africa, and Puerto Rico and sing to the world and all those who lived in it. In the future I wanted to adopt African and Chinese children and bring them to America to live out their American Dream just like I was doing. I knew I couldn't adopt every child suffering, but with just one or two I would feel like I put my stamp on the world no matter how these children turned out. I would never turn my back on them and I would assist them through any difficulty that they faced while I was alive.

Of course I wanted my own children, but we would all mix in together as one big happy family. I hoped I could convince Ronnie to want the same dreams as I did, but he didn't and he wouldn't make a commitment to me. He was the only guy I was with and I prayed that I was the only woman he was with. He had never said the words to let me know that he wanted to be with just me. I was guessing he didn't, because as we got to know each other we found out that we were so different. I knew this going into it, but there was something about him that made me want more than just a friendship with this man. Now I was caught up in a relationship that I wasn't sure if I would be in any longer. I needed to probably focus on school. Maybe if I eased up a little on the singing with the band and took a break from seeing Ronnie things would work it self out. I didn't know what I was going to do, but I had a few weeks to decide. I just hoped that come the New Year I would have made the right decision. I was alright for the moment.

It was Friday night. Kenya, Dontae and I were going out for dinner, then to Republic Garden for a night of dancing. I had asked Ronnie if he wanted to come. He said he may swing by after going to watch a "Go-Go" band at the Reeves Center. I knew all that meant was: call me when you finished hanging with your friends. Ronnie never wanted to hang with the three of us. I guessed I couldn't really blame him: he was the eclectic, artsy type, and my friends were all caught up in school, opening up businesses and becoming lawyers. I could see how it could be boring to him, but I did wish he and I had more in common outside the band and the bedroom. I must say that he was an awesome lover, so once I was done chilling with my people I would be walking my ass over to the Reeves Center.

AFTER I MET UP WITH RONNIE we went back to my place and picked up my luggage. He was taking me to the airport in the morning and we were going back to his place. I had already bought his Christmas gift and wrapped it before going out that night. I bought him a gold and platinum bracelet from Zales, a jewelry store at the mall. I knew he was going to like it, because one thing I had learned about him since I met him was that he loved jewelry. That was something we did have in common. He carried my bags back to his Cadillac and I handed him his gift; I told him he could open it up when we got back to his place if he wanted, or he could wait until Christmas and call me and let me know what he thought.

He said he would decide once we got back to his place. When he got in the car I asked him one more time if he wanted to come to NYC and spend Christmas with me, my dad and his wife. I knew he didn't have that much family and the thought of someone that I loved spending Christmas alone didn't feel right to me. However, Ronnie was so stubborn, though, and moved to the beat of his own drum. There was no convincing him to do anything thing that he didn't want to do.

This was what bugged me the most about him, because I always thought the person who I would fall in love with: he and I would act as a team together, and that compromise and consideration would be the fabric that held us together. But I couldn't get this man to do anything that he didn't want to do. It didn't matter how much I wanted it or how passionate I was about something, if he didn't like it, then he wouldn't do it.

This really pissed me off and it was starting to become unbearable. I felt like he was pushing me away, but wouldn't just walk away. I could depend on him when I was feeling lonely. All I had to do was call him and he would be over my apartment teaching me a new song, holding me, kissing me, and making love to me, but then for about a week he was distant, mean and barely had anything to say to me. He acted all business-like. I had never felt like this before and I knew I had a lot to think about over the break, as far as whether I was going to continue the relationship or walk away before it got ugly.

I heard that in August American Idol was coming to D.C. for auditions. I had met this woman who worked for a local radio station at the club tonight. She had watched me perform before and said she could get me an audition if I was interested. I was very excited about this opportunity; I loved American Idol and was glued to the television when it came on. This was a way out of this emotionally abusive relationship and thank goodness I could go back to school. I was able to pass every single one of my classes. School and doing my own thing singing would keep me from not being so worried about making things work between Ronnie and I, I had hoped.

The night with Ronnie went as usual. We had another night of passionate love-making. He made my body feel ecstatic but as soon as it was over he got up, took a shower, came back in the bed and fell right to sleep. There was no cuddling, holding or pillow talk. He decided not to open up his present and when we woke up the next morning he took me to the airport, kissed me and handed me a card with my name printed on the front with his handwriting. I was kind of disappointed because I was hoping he had picked something out for me that would make me feel like he truly cared about me. Since I didn't read the card nor did I know what was in it, I decided to just kiss him goodbye, wished him a merry Christmas, and walked away and into the airport.

I needed my daddy right now, I thought while I took the hour flight into NYC. He always knew how to make me feel good. He washed all my worries away and made me feel like I was the only girl in the world. I could lay my head on his lap and without even knowing all my problems, he could see through me. He knew just the right words to say to make me feel confident in making the choices that would guide me in the right direction.

As soon as I walked off the plane I picked up my luggage from baggage claim, headed out JFK to my smiling father who had the door open to the backseat of his Lincoln.

"Hey baby girl, I feel like it has been decades since I have seen you. I think you came home more often when you were further away in Atlanta. I know there must be someone special in your life, and I was hoping you would be bringing him with you so I could meet him finally."

Damn, I thought, I couldn't keep anything from this man; he knew me like a book. I hugged him and we both got in the backseat of the car. "Well daddy, there is this guy that I have been dating for several months down in D.C.," I confessed in a whisper. I knew he would be able to hear me. I didn't want to say it too loud because there was still no confirmation that I was actually Ronnie's girl. "I don't know where things are going between us right now. Things are not as great as they could be, and it has me pretty down at the moment. But this is our time together so let's enjoy it." I really didn't feel like discussing Ronnie right now.

"Now you know you can't keep anything from me, I know you as well as I know myself. Believe it or not, you are the male version of me. Every time I see you I can see me. I will wait until you feel more comfortable talking about this fellow, but just remember you are too special of a person to have to deal with someone that isn't treating you right."

"I know daddy … I know … It's just hard when you want something so bad, and that person will not give it to you."

"Well sweetheart you deserve anything you want so don't settle for anybody not willing to give you what your heart desires, and I mean that. I don't ever want to see you caught up with the wrong person. People can bring you down and change you for the worst. I will have someone removed from this earth before I let some man ruin my daughter's life."

I knew he meant just that. My father had always been the overprotective type, which was why I never confided in him about the rape incident with Cordel when I was on spring break. My father had the know-how and the means to get rid of someone and as much as I wanted Cordel to suffer, I couldn't live with myself with his blood on my hands. Plus I didn't want daddy to look at me like I was vulnerable. He always thought I was much smarter and stronger then I felt I really was. This was something I began to realize about myself, that I always had people fooled. Most people would think I had everything together, because I was smart, pretty and talented, but if you really got to know me, you would see that I was just as vulnerable as the next person. I just did a good job of not showing my weaknesses, I guess.

"Well baby girl, I have an exciting Christmas eve planned for the both of us. We are going to go back to the condo in Manhattan so you can freshen up, then we are going to go to Central Park and watch a variety-show fundraiser that the kids of the Harlem Performing Arts School are throwing. There is going to be good singing, dancing, and I know you will be excited to see their fashion show. Then after that we are going to meet up with Veronica for a bite to eat at her favorite restaurant in Soho. She is excited to see you. She has been doing a lot of shopping for things that she thinks you might like."

"Well that sounds like fun, daddy. And when I see Veronica I am going to have to let her know that she needs to stop trying so hard. She doesn't need to suck up to me. I like her because you love her."

"I know baby, but she just wants to be your friend and she wants you to like her that's all."

We were already running late so I changed real fast, applied some more makeup and dressed warm since we were going to be outside. We headed right back out the door. When we pulled up to the park daddy and I walked up to the front to the VIP section where there were chairs and hors d'oeuvres. Most of the people who came out to support the kids stood up on the grass behind the VIP section. Although I was sure daddy's company gave generously to the school, I knew he had an agenda. He was looking for some fresh new talent and he was in the right place because these kids were good.

There was this young guy who really stood out – he couldn't have been more than fifteen. He had a real nice deep strong voice, though, and when you closed your eyes you would think a grown man was singing. He did the best rendition of Silent Night that I ever heard in my life. I looked over to see my father while he was singing. I could tell he was thinking "gold mine" as this young man was going through his version of this famous Christmas song. The fashion show was the last segment of the show and the models looked grown; I could hardly believe that these were teenagers. I didn't know what they put in the food these days because these girls looked like they just stepped out of Italian Vogue.

After the show daddy introduced me to some of the faculty and members who were on the school's board of trustees, mostly Alumni and they too were in the entertainment business. Daddy introduced me as his smart daughter in law school who wanted no part of the "business" – so he thought. I still felt bad keeping my newfound interest from daddy; I knew he would be hurt once he found out. But he would just have to understand that I wanted to do things my way. I didn't want anything handed to me. If I was going to have a successful career I was going to do it my way, and on my own terms.

We left the show after mingling for a while and went to go meet my stepmother, who was only a couple years older than I was. She too was an aspiring singer and had been part of a girl group that had one popular hit back when I was a freshman. Now she sang back up for people like Mary J. Blige, Faith Evans, and whoever had a hit song out. Her career slowed down after she got married to my father though. She spent a lot of time spending his money shopping and going on trips with her friends. Why my dad was in love with this woman I would never know, but something tells me he was a little pussy-whipped.

When we walked into the small quaint French restaurant where we would be spending our Christmas Eve, Veronica was sitting at a table that had three placements setup. When we walked up to the table she stood up and hugged me and daddy. I greeted her with a smile and she did the same. She looked real good – her hair was freshly done and her makeup was flawless. She was wearing a stylish Donna Karan purple pants suit with gold Manolo Blahnik pumps. She was dressed like she was a woman in her thirties, but I knew her real age – only twenty-five. I told myself that I would be nice and not make her feel uncomfortable.

"Veronica, I love those shoes you're wearing. I almost bought the same pair back in D.C., but they didn't have my size," I complimented.

"Thank you Jennifer, I just picked these up yesterday. Had I known we had the same taste I would have gotten you a pair as well."

"Well you don't have to do that, but thanks. This is a really nice restaurant that you picked out for the three of us."

"I am glad you like it. After spending a month in Paris for our honeymoon I came back to America missing all the great French foods that your father introduced me to. I have been coming here every month, sometimes twice since I left Paris because the food here is very authentic." I tried not to laugh, but I thought that was the most ridiculous thing I heard and I tried real hard to hold back my laughter. I had been to Paris and the food was not all that. Daddy could tell that I was amused by just looking in my eyes and he reached under the table and squeezed my leg. I knew this meant for me to calm down.

I really didn't like spending a lot of time with Veronica. She had the tendency to talk about herself too much. It almost felt like she had something to prove to me and she tended to dominate the conversation, cutting me off when I was speaking. I really didn't have the energy to deal with this tonight. I had too much on my mind. So as she went on and on about how much volunteer work she had been doing since she'd been married and how she'd been able to help her family out since my dad was so generous. I kind of tuned her out and thought about who I would be married to in the future. Veronica liked to hear herself talk so much she didn't even realize that I wasn't listening to her anymore.

When we finished our dinner and the waitress asked if we wanted dessert and coffee, I spoke up and told everyone that I was kind of tired. I was ready to call it a night. I knew Veronica wasn't really ready to go but since she was trying to suck up to me, she didn't protest. Daddy paid for the dinner and we all got in the Lincoln to go uptown to daddy's condo.

When we got back to the house and I finished unpacking the clothes I had brought for these two days and put the gifts I bought for Daddy and Veronica underneath the tree. I could tell daddy had nothing to do with the choice of the tree because ordinarily it would be fake, and out of a Macy's catalog with a three-color-toned scheme. Not this tree; it went all the way to the top of the ceiling and had every color of the rainbow on it, with candy canes and different miniature pieces of black baby dolls. This was definitely not my daddy's style nor mine for that matter. This tree had way too much going on, it looked gaudy. Veronica must had gone crazy in the store and just bought everything.

It was getting kind of late and I knew daddy was in the living room watching the news. I didn't know what Veronica was doing so I decided to lay on the bed and open the card that Ronnie had given me for Christmas. The card had a black Santa Claus on the front and said, "If you could ask Santa to bring you anything for Christmas, what would it be?" Then the inside read, "Hopefully, it would be friends, family and a healthy life." I thought this was very generic and it didn't tell me how he felt about me, but then I noticed there was a letter that was written in his hand writing on it that read, "Unfold me." And I did.

Dear J.P.,

You are a special person and I am glad that we have gotten the chance to get to know each other. However, I think that we are moving too fast and you want something right now that I am unable to give you. I don't know if it is because of my past and me having a hard time getting close to people. But I feel that every day that is passing I am holding you back from living the life that you are destined to be fulfilling. You do not belong in my band. I knew this when I first heard you sing, but there was something about you that I couldn't pass up the opportunity of getting to know. I had no idea that you would fall for someone like me as fast as you did, and I didn't want to hurt you so I went with the flow. I know there is a man out there that deserves you and who will treat you better than I could ever. Please do not hate me, and I hope that you and I can be friends. This is one of the hardest things I had to do, but I cannot continue to keep a beautiful dove from flying. Maybe I am making the wrong decision and jumping to conclusions, but I would like to disassemble the band after our New Year's Eve performance. Enjoy your family during the Holidays and know that I care for you a lot.

Love Ronnie

I was in tears as I sat the letter on the bed. I was trying not to sob, because I didn't want daddy or Veronica to hear me. As much as I knew that the ending of our relationship was inevitable, I didn't know why Ronnie couldn't love me and make me happy. This amount of rejection was kind of hard to bear and I didn't know how to deal with it. One minute I was thinking about calling him and begging him to try to work this out with me, and the next minute I was like fuck that motherfucker, if he can't see a diamond in the rough, then good riddance.

I asked God that night, "What are You trying to tell me?" Why would He let me find this man and fall in love with him and not allow him to fall in love with me? I started to feel like something was wrong with me. Maybe I was too depressed from my mother passing that I couldn't open up to be loved. I would always live with the pain of being hurt and rejected by someone who I really wanted to love me and take care of me. I guess this was how my mother must have felt when my father walked out on her. I knew one thing, though: Ronnie was not the man that was going to make me want to end my life.

In order for me to get to sleep I had to look at things on the bright side. He did help me find my passion, singing. I didn't have to give that up, but he was kicking me out the group, and I was sure New Years Eve would be our last performance together. I knew then that I wanted to continue singing and I guessed now I would have to pave my own path and not hide behind Ronnie and his band. It sucked because I was just starting to like it. Oh, well, I would just practice and do all I needed to do to perform well on my audition with American Idol. Even if Carol, the lady I met last night, wasn't able to come through for me, I was sure Kenya would wait outside in line with me all night and day until I made Paula, Randy and Simon hear me sing.

Ronnie basically left me hanging with that letter, but I didn't let this ruin my Christmas with my father. When I woke up the next morning daddy had breakfast made; I could smell the eggs and bacon from my bedroom. I jumped up, took a shower, put my hair in a pony tail and threw on some sweats and walked out to Veronica and Daddy sitting in the dining room drinking coffee and talking.

"Hey, I thought I was going to have to come in there and wake you up so we can start opening up gifts. Normally you are up before I am. Is everything okay, baby?"

"Yes daddy, I am fine, I guess I was just catching up on my rest from all the late-night studying and cramming for finals. Let's see what everyone got for Christmas." There was so much under the tree that it took us over two hours to finish unwrapping every gift. I had way too much stuff to take back to D.C. Daddy said he would make sure everything got shipped down to me next week, which was something he did every year. With Veronica going out of her way to please me I had more things than I had ever gotten for Christmas, and Daddy had never been cheap. She went crazy with designer scarves, necklaces, makeup, and perfume. I could go on and on. I had only gotten her a Louis Vuitton scarf, gloves and hat set that I got from Barney's. She said she liked it a lot and was glad that I had thought about her. Of course Daddy did have to remind me that it would be nice if I picked up something nice for Veronica for Christmas about two weeks ago.

The three of us got dressed and went out to Times Square for a day of ice skating and ice cream. That was a ritual of daddy's and mine for as long as I could remember. I remembered growing up and every Christmas I would wish that I would grow up to be the next Oksana Baiul or Nancy Kerrigan, but unfortunately ice skating lessons never seemed appealing once the spring and summer came along. Even though I was a pretty good ice skater I never got to be good enough for competition skating.

After skating we headed over to our relatives and Veronica's family to drop off gifts and receive some more things that I had to get shipped to me in D.C. We first went over to my grandmother's house, my father's mothers. Daddy bought her a real big house in Connecticut in the suburbs of New York City years ago. We had Christmas dinner in this house for as long as I could remember. I remembered as a child coming up here with my mother and daddy. I was a little girl with no cares in the world, excited to go play with my cousins and all the kids who lived in granny's neighborhood. We would be outside racing new remote-control cars or learning how to ride new bikes that we'd just got for Christmas.

Now that I was older I got to see all my cousins' children, and some of the kids who used to live there came back to their parents' houses with their families to enjoy Christmas. Christmas had a way of making people feel good. I never in my life met anyone who was having a bad day on Christmas. I was not saying that people didn't, but I had seen the meanest people all of sudden turn nice during the Christmas season. After we spent time with our half of the family, we went to the hood in Brooklyn to visit Veronica's side of the family.

Her mother – we called her Miss Mable – still lived in the projects in Canarsie. She was the type of women who was set in her ways. After Veronica married my father they offered her a place in a three-bedroom brownstone my father rented in Spanish Harlem. He had just spent over a hundred thousand dollars in renovations; and it had a new kitchen, bathroom and hardwood floors throughout. She said she was comfortable where she was, having lived in the same apartment for over twenty years, and didn't want to move away from her friends. At first I had kind of understood where she was coming from, but after visiting this hellhole, I would've been on the next thing smoking out of Brooklyn. She had mousetraps everywhere, and I saw roaches in every part of the apartment.

We hadn't planned on staying long, just long enough to drop off presents and spend a little time with her family. Veronica had three older sisters who all had kids by fathers who were either in jail or didn't have anything to do with their children. Her eldest daughter still lived at home with her two kids. My father was like Santa Claus to their family; he splurged on every single nephew and niece Veronica had. I didn't really have a problem with this because these kids didn't have a choice growing up poor, and daddy had more than enough to share with six underprivileged kids. I could tell that Veronica's older sister was very jealous of her when I met her at the wedding. She refused to be a bridesmaid, let alone the maid of honor. She told me her sister had been a gold-digger since junior high school. I kept this information to myself, because daddy was happy and I didn't know what Stacy's motivation was for telling me this information.

When daddy brought the gifts into the apartment for the kids, Stacy made a comment to Veronica that she was always showing off and trying to outdo everyone. Of course Veronica got pissed and they started fussing back and forth. Miss Mable shut them both down and reminded them that it was Christmas and it was meant for the kids. She said they needed to get over any sibling rivalry they had immediately. And when Miss Mable talked, you had better shut up. She was one of those large women with a big voice who was probably a man-eater in her day. Daddy grabbed Veronica by her waist and sat her down on his lap in an attempt to quiet her down as well. The kids just watched with their mouths open. You could tell they had witnessed the two of them arguing before.

I was a little bit jealous of Veronica because I had never experienced this before with a sibling, being an only child. I admired her as well because now that she'd married someone with money, she didn't forget about her family. She'd always made an effort to make sure her nieces and nephews didn't want for anything. She even got her oldest niece into the Harlem Performing Arts School on a full scholarship, using some of my father's connections. It was sad that her older sister Stacy couldn't look at this as more of an opportunity than as Veronica trying to show off her newfound fortune. We stayed a little less then an hour before we made our way back to Manhattan.

When we had got back to the condo I packed my things and took out what I would be wearing to the airport tomorrow so I could head back to D.C. Daddy was trying to convince me to stay longer, knowing I had two weeks before school started, but I told him that I had prior commitments with friends and that I really needed to get back to D.C. I kind of did want to stay longer because these two days had went by really fast and being around daddy made me feel special, but I needed to close these loose ends with Ronnie and start practicing for my last performance with the band. Ronnie was supposed to pick me up but I sent him a text letting him know that I would get home from the airport by myself and that I would be at his house on time for rehearsal on Tuesday.

He sent me a text back asking if I was sure and that he didn't mind, but he understood. I didn't even respond. I just called Kenya and let her know what time I would be arriving and she said that it was no problem. She was on vacation the entire week. She said to call her if anything changed and she would be there on time to pick me up. Again I had to be thankful that she was back in my life because I knew her friendship would be very therapeutic in the days of trying to get over Ronnie.

Kenya was one of those folks who had to be in the mall the day after Christmas for the after-Christmas bargains. I thought this was all a hoax, because now that the day had become so popular stores have gotten the clue and don't actually lower the prices until the week after Christmas. I said what the hell, shopping was relaxing and I needed to drop the bomb to Kenya about Ronnie anyway. Why not do it at the mall? We had both spent way too much money in Nordstrom, where we spent almost two hours trying on clothes and shoes and getting makeovers and smelling perfume. I actually felt relaxed and fulfilled when we were done. We ended up going for a late lunch after shopping. I had already dropped the bomb about Ronnie when we were in the dressing room trying on clothes. She looked shocked by the news but was too busy with the clothes to spend that much time on it, but she promised drinks and dinner after shopping to spill my guts and I would have her undivided attention.

The next question was, "How does my butt look in this skirt," and the subject was changed instantly.

Now that we were sitting down at Champs, sipping on Mojitos, it was all about me. I handed her the letter that he wrote and sipped my drink while she read the letter intently. She was very silent while she read, not giving me any inclination as to how she felt. When she was finished reading the letter, she handed it back to me and I put it in my purse.

"Well, to be honest with you Ronnie sounds like a wimp. That is all his letter boils down to in its entirety," Kenya told me as she sighed real hard. Kenya had a lot more insight than I did, having grown up in Brooklyn and raised by her grandmother, she was old beyond her young years.

"What do you mean?" I looked at her puzzled.

"Well J.P., first off this man has some really serious issues that he needs to deal with. Nobody in their right mind ends a relationship in a letter. I know you have mentioned to me before that he won't commit to you, but he did, in his own way. If he didn't then there would be no need for this letter. Appearance is everything and you two were committed, but you know what your problem is?"

"What is my problem?"

"I was getting to that before you interrupted me my dear. Your problem is you are too strong of a woman for these men you date because of how you were brought up. Your daddy has millions of dollars to buy you anything you need, you have a trust fund. The ordinary man especially the black man who barely can pay his rent, let alone buy a home feels like he can't do anything to please you because you have everything. I am your best friend and when I first met you I thought you could be a little spoiled and snobby. I know I was mean just now, but let me finish. All I can say is you used to be all over the place when I met you in college. Now you are focused and you know what you want to do and it is great seeing you like this. I have never seen you like this before and I love it; you are finally showing some vulnerability."

"Wait a minute, now you are sounding contradictory; how can I be intimidating in one breath and vulnerable in the next?"

"Well don't get me wrong, you have changed in my eyes, but we are only friends. Being your best friend, the only advice I can give you is you are going to have to find a man who is strong and can deal with a strong personality. If I were you I wouldn't worry about it. Any man who is not fighting to be with you is a man who is not worthy enough to be with you. I can see why you like Ronnie; he is definitely fine and he looks like he is a good lover. However, you deserve more and I hope that you find the right man for you."

"Thanks baby and I hope you do the same. You make a lot of sense; there is just going to be emptiness inside me for a while, because he has been constant in my life. And the fact that he doesn't want to be with me, I should just move on. I know I can't focus on someone who doesn't want to be with me. No matter how intriguing I find this man, everyone in this world should be able to be with the person that they mutually and exclusively want to be with. You know what I mean?"

"Now you know I know what you mean, J.P., and trust me, you will find the man of your dreams. You might be too large for Ronnie, too much woman for him." I needed to hear those words to get me pumped up an excited about meeting someone who would truly be right for me. I was kind of exhausted with everything that had been going on and tired of talking about this with my homegirl. Kenya put things back into perspective for me and I was now ready to move on and see what else life had in store for me. We had a few drinks and Kenya dropped me off at my crib. I checked my voicemail and I had three messages: one from daddy making sure I got back to D.C. safely, the next was from Dontae hoping I had a merry Christmas and said he was still in Seattle visiting his family but he would be back in a couple of days, and the last message was from Ronnie, stating that he wanted to make sure that I got back to D.C. and to give him a call.

I decided to return everyone's call but Ronnie's. We had rehearsal tomorrow, so I would just see him then, no need to get all emotional again. I was a big girl, so he needed to know I would be just fine. After I unpacked my bags I went to my bedroom to take a nap, and I noticed that the light on my voicemail to my home phone was lit. Nobody usually called me on this phone. I was surprised to see that I had a message. When I pressed the button to listen to the message I was shocked at the familiar voice that resonated out the machine.

"I hope this message finds you well, Jennifer. I had to resort to the old-fashioned white pages to look you up. I tried calling your sorority sister Candice to get your number but she said she lost her phone while she was doing some modeling in Europe and couldn't give me the number. Anyway, I am in D.C. this week, training and meeting up with some agents. I left Philly today visiting my family and I knew you moved to D.C., so I thought we could hang. Please call me when you get the message, my number is (267) 555-1423, and I look forward to hearing from you and possibly seeing you again."

Hearing Kurt's voice gave me goose bumps. I had a really big crush on him when I stayed at his crib for spring break, and I could swear he was flirting with me. However, since Cordel messed up everything, we didn't get a chance to exchange numbers or spend any time together at the party. Since he was in D.C., I was very excited to see what he was up to. I was always told one way to get over one man is to get under another one, and wow, Kurt had impeccable timing.

CHAPTER 8

Dontae

I was at the car auction excited that I would be finally getting some wheels. "We have a 1996 Pontiac Grand Am for $1500 hundred going once going twice sold to number 65. Remember cash, credit cards or money orders are the only monetary funds we accept." The auctioneer moved on to the next vehicle he was trying to dispose of today. I finally had saved up three thousand dollars to purchase a vehicle to get me around town. I couldn't believe people said you could get around D.C. without a car. I had my eye on this 1997 Acura Legend that I was checking out before the auction started and I couldn't wait until it was time for it to be presented. It was all black with leather interior, sun roof, and it had a five-disk CD changer located behind the passenger seat. The tag said it was seized in a drug bust and it had all its paperwork. It had just been through inspection, so all I needed to do was get the title changed and it was mine. I also had to outbid everyone else though. We came on a Wednesday. Darrel said it was slower than on the weekend and I would have more chances of getting what I wanted, since it would be less crowded. We both skipped our afternoon classes and drove to Timonium, which is past Baltimore. J.P. and I still had all the same courses this semester so she promised to fill me in on what I had missed after I came back with my new car.

The auctioneer must have called off about ten cars before he got to the one I was interested in. He started introducing all the features and started the car off at only $1,000. I thought it would be nice if I could get the car for that amount, but of course it was just my luck that I went back and forth with this older white lady until she outbid me for $4,000. I was kind of pissed, because I really wanted that car but about three cars later I settled for a two-door 1998 Honda Accord. It was silver with a sunroof, and factory CD player. It lacked leather seats but it was in really nice condition and I was satisfied with my choice. I only ended up paying $2,300 for it, so I saved a little bit of money in the process. Boy was I excited to be back behind the wheel again, having given up my car back home because it was an old 1980 Datsun. They didn't even make Datsuns anymore. There was no way it would have made it the 3000 miles to D.C. I felt so liberated following Darrel back into the city driving my own vehicle. All I could think about was I could finally afford to sleep in, because being able to drive to school would take time off my commute.

My grandmother always told me that a car was a liability, more trouble then it was worth, and boy did I know that. The first week I got my driver's license I got into an accident and within the first year I had my license I was in three accidents. Only one wasn't my fault. Not to mention all the parking tickets that I racked up on my college campus, running late for classes and parking in areas where I knew I wasn't supposed to park. The parking situation was much worse in D.C., so with the money I saved I planned on biting the bullet and purchasing on-campus parking, which was way too much, $300 a semester. So yeah, granny was right: driving was an expensive liability; you have to get insurance and you had to have a place to park the car, not to mention maintenance and gas. This was one liability that I welcomed with pleasure. No more waiting for the bus and then the train. No more crowded buses, homeless folks asking me for change every day. I could come and go as I pleased and I was happy.

Darrel promised to take me out to dinner tonight to celebrate once we got back in the city. The funny thing was that I wasn't remotely hungry, because I was so high off of having my own whip. When we got to the restaurant all I ordered was a chicken salad. I only ate a couple of bites and took it home with me. Darrel and I had gotten real close since our trip to Atlantic City, which was the bomb. We made love the whole weekend. We only went out one time to gamble and he showed me how to play blackjack at the tables. I ended up losing forty dollars on the five-dollar table and he won about a hundred and fifty dollars. Gambling kind of gave me a rush and I knew I needed to stay away from the casinos because I could see I could lose a lot of money in that place if I wasn't careful.

Since coming back for Atlantic City I spent most nights over Darrel's place, which I enjoyed because Jemal had gotten worse now that I had a steady boyfriend. I didn't know if he was jealous because he didn't have anybody or if he wanted to be with me. There was so much tension in that small apartment when we were both there that I tried my best to stay in my room whenever he was home. I knew I wouldn't be staying there another year unless things got better, and honestly I didn't see that happening.

Now that I had gotten the hang of law school and all this damn reading that was required, it gave me more free time to actually enjoy the city more. Darrel and I would go out on the weekends to a club or a house party, which D.C. usually had one or two going on. One thing I could say was that the gay folks liked to throw a party. Darrel always knew what was going on, which made me jealous a little bit because sometimes when I wanted to stay in and study and I wanted him to stay in with me, he just had to be out on the town. I hoped and prayed that he was loyal when he went out without me. Every time I did go out he made it an effort to let everyone know that he had a boyfriend which was me, so that gave me a little bit of solace. Darrel was extremely friendly, and very attractive, so I knew he got hit on when I wasn't around, coupled with the fact that having a boyfriend made you more appealing in the eyes of the desperate.

Midterms for the second semester were over and next week we had interviews scheduled on campus with recruiters from law firms, non-profit organizations and associations mainly from, D.C., New York, Chicago, Los Angeles and Miami lined up for summer internships. Being that I was in the top five percentile of my class and I was African-American, I had several interviews lined up next week. I was really excited because since I had done so well the first semester, everyone told me that I pretty much could pick and choose where I wanted to be this summer. I even had an interview lined up with a firm back home in Seattle that wanted to interview me. I didn't know why I even signed up for this because I knew I wouldn't be spending my summer in Seattle. I just left that place and I was not ready to go home, especially not for the summer. Most folks who did as well as I did usually went to New York to work for one of the top firms. I was contemplating going up for the summer. Any job I take the pay was going to be good, so I just had to impress the people that I interviewed with and hopefully make a decision in the upcoming month.

For the next several days leading up to the interviews, I was still on cloud nine since I was mobile and on the road. I felt like I was finally doing my thing. Everything was happening as planned, I was doing well in school, found a part-time job and was making a few coins. I wasn't on the prowl looking for a boyfriend because I had found somebody I was attracted to who I felt was equally attracted to me and it was working out lovely. Now all I needed to do was land me a fierce internship and summer location to further work out my plans. My first day of interviews was with five firms, I decided not take any interviews with private companies, the government or any associations. I wanted to work in a law firm and actually experience the whole ordeal. I've had jobs before, and even though I would be practicing law, a job was a job. I wanted to experience what I set out to do, in a setting with people who wanted to do exactly what I wanted to do, and have gone through schooling and knew the laws and how to practice them. So I declined every interview except the ones with actual law firms. I had interviews scheduled all week long and for the most part I think I knocked every single one of them out. My top three choices were two firms in New York City and the other firm was in Washington, D.C. The only reason I was even considering staying was Darrel, the federal government was paying his full tuition and starting this summer he had to intern with the Department of Justice. He also had to give them three years of service after he graduated. I thought that was a sweet deal for him; the government paid for everything and even though he would only be making about ninety-five thousand a year he had no expensive law school bills like most lawyers, which was the reason why it was a must to make a six-figure-plus salary.

The following month I decided to stay in D.C. and work with one of the top firms here that did legal work for politicians who were running for office. The first black man who had a shot of winning the presidency retained the firm and they offered me triple the pay to work for them this summer. I really had my heart set on working in NYC, but the pay was just too much to pass on. I would be getting five thousand a week, plus car service at night if I stayed after seven. There were only two spots available at this firm for interns with this pay and the rest only received twenty-five hundred a week, with no perks, so it paid to do well the first semester.

I was really excited to see a black man running for president; many people didn't think America was ready for this type of change, having a black man running the country. We had been appointed CEOs of Fortune 500 companies, we are mayors, senators, congressmen and governors; why not the president of the United States? Blacks had been a very vital part of American history, so I think now was a better time than ever – and I wanted to do my part – to see it happen, so I jumped on the opportunity to work with this firm who could potentially represent the first black president.

I passed my midterms with flying colors and I was slated to continue being in the top of my class. The way I studied I felt I should have been number one, but G.U. is so competitive that there were students who studied way more than I did, to the point where they had no life and there were times when I felt that way. Right after midterms my good luck kind of hit the fan. Darrel's father had a stroke during the Easter weekend and he was back and forth from D.C. to the Eastern Shore every free moment he got. It got to the point where it had been two weeks before I had seen him, and I was missing him, but I knew I couldn't complain because of the situation. Then one dreadful night he came by on a Sunday at three a.m. and said that his fathered had passed. There was nothing the doctors could do to save him. I comforted him that night and we made love so passionately that I knew he was the one for me. He cried throughout the whole night and I just held him tight and said it would be okay.

Darrel and his father were really close. Although he kept the fact that he was gay from his father, they still talked about everything else. He confessed to me that his father told him the last time they talked that he needed to find a nice woman, to settle down with, once he finished law school. He said he knew about his other life, and that he had gone through the same thing when he was his age. It was nothing but heartache and pain and he didn't want him to live his life like that and he had to promise him that he would give it all up. When he confessed this to me I immediately got scared, and was hoping that he didn't plan to fulfill his father's dying wishes. I had experienced the most electrifying and satisfying moments the last seven months with somebody I could see myself spending the rest of my life with and he was now contemplating whether or not he wanted to be with a man or woman for the rest of his life.

I didn't say much that night, I just held him tight and let my shoulder be a safe place to cry and lean on in his time of need. Darrel didn't call me after he left for the next two days and I was getting nervous and worried that maybe he decided to do what his father had asked him to do. I found the obituary in the Eastern Shore Daily Chronicle while surfing on the Internet. It gave the time and location of his father's funeral and I decided to miss my Friday classes and drove down on my own. Darrel still wasn't returning my calls, so when I got to the funeral I decided to sit in the back where nobody could see me. I saw Darrel and his family sitting in the front pew of the church. I also saw Darrel holding the same girl that I had seen in his prom picture and several other pictures he had in a photo album at his place. He told me that she was his high school sweetheart and everyone thought they would one day get married, but he left her behind to go to college and then to law school. I felt like I wanted to throw up when I recognized it was her. I wanted to be down there comforting him and holding him. I knew in a perfect world I would have been able to, but in the world we lived in, I had to sit in the shadow, like the invisible man, not showing his family or the world that I loved this man more than anyone could possibly know. I could never do it in public and this hurt me deeply. I left the service before it began and got in my car and cried in the parking lot for thirty minutes until I got myself together to take the drive back to D.C.

Somehow I knew things were going too good to be true. I finished the semester without even talking to Darrel. I called him every day for about a month, until one day his number was disconnected. It took everything not to go to his school and look for him and ask for an explanation, but I wasn't a stalker. If he wanted to just walk out on me then there was nothing I was going to do about it to protest. I had been through too much in my life to let an individual bring me down. So I was in denial for the months that passed, I put all my energy into my schoolwork. I wasn't dating or going out or anything. My living arrangement with Jemal got better during this time as well. We decided to go to Puerto Rico during Memorial Day weekend on a vacation and during this time there was an event going on called San Juan Brothers, where a lot of black gay men from around the country came to the island to party and enjoy the sun. David and a few of his friends were down there this weekend too, so we all had a blast, enjoying the clubs, and going to the beach.

During my time in Puerto Rico, I met a guy name Omar from Atlanta who was very attractive. He was thirty-two, which was almost ten years older than I was, but he looked more like twenty-five. I still had Darrel on my mind, but Omar did a really good job of helping me forget that I was once in love with Darrel. The last night after a long night of dancing and partying, I went back to his suite at the Marriot and one thing led to another and I ended up going all the way with him sexually. I really didn't come to the island for this, but hey, it had been a minute, and I had my needs too. I knew I would never talk to this guy again, since we lived in two different cities. Since I was on vacation and I had used protection I was like what the hell.

Puerto Rico was a great getaway and I had worked really hard during my first year in law school. When I got back to D.C., I started my internship which from day one was very demanding. I had to be at work at eight a.m. every morning, and most days I stayed until ten at night. My job consisted mostly of research on primary laws and logistics on the upcoming primaries that our candidate had left. The partner in charge of our work mentioned to us in orientation that normally we wouldn't be working as hard during this time of year because the nominee would have been chosen by now. But since it was a very close race we had to spend as much time making sure that we knew every inside of every law that the state had to distribute its allotted delegates to the Democratic convention. We had various political consultants working for the firm as well assisting us with the research.

I didn't get a chance to breathe or anything until the fourth of July. I did, however, enjoy a little bit of break. My birthday was in June – I was a Gemini – so J.P. took me out to eat and celebrate. She was working for the same law firm I was as a volunteer; unfortunately her grades weren't as high as mine so she wasn't offered a paid position. Since we felt the same way about the possibility of there becoming a black president, she felt she wanted to help out as much as she could for the cause. So after work on my birthday we went to the Cheesecake Factory and got twisted. We both came into work late the next morning, but since everyone knew yesterday was my birthday nobody really said anything. For the 4th of July I took my next trip. This time it was to California for the gay beach party; it was actually Los Angeles' black gay pride as well. This time just David and I went on this trip.

David and I had become real close; we had a lot in common and he reminded me of my friend Lonnie that I used to hang around back in Seattle right before I moved. Lonnie was the caregiver type of friend. He was the kind of person who did any and everything you asked him to do. When I was moving to D.C. my grandmother asked me what I was going to do without Lonnie while I was packing. I wasn't even thinking about the fact that I would miss him; I was just ready to move on with my life and embark on some new shit. I responded so arrogantly and egotistically that I didn't even know how Lonnie or my Grandmother felt about my answer, really, because they didn't comment. But I said, "I'll find another Lonnie," as if it would be that easy to find someone to replace that good of a friend, and trust me I had never found another friend like him in my life and I realized now that true friends were priceless.

Lonnie and his boyfriend Keith had moved to Los Angeles after I moved to D.C. The couple of times I talked to Lonnie while I'd been in D.C., he told me that they loved living in L.A. He constantly bragged about the weather, going to the beach and all the celebrities that he had met. We all hung out when David and I got to L.A. They met us at the Westin

Hotel where we were staying, which was the host hotel for the pride event. Lonnie was kind of relentless when it came to men, even though he had a man and his man treated him really well. In fact I kind of had a crush on Keith when I first met him, and was kind of sad when he picked my best friend over me.

Anyway, Lonnie flirted and had sex with anyone he chose to, of course behind Keith's back. I think he wasn't really all that into Keith, but he represented security and someone who would put up with his crap and take care of him. One thing I noticed about Lonnie being his best friend was that he was very dependent. I think we all were in a way, but some folks had it bad. It was like they couldn't function without someone else being by their side. He was my best friend and I loved him to death, but he was irritating me by flirting with David. I didn't want to be in the middle of a love triangle with two friends. But knowing a little bit about David, although Lonnie was really cute he wasn't exactly David's type. David was into the real masculine, thuggish type dudes.

The four of us went to the beach party together and there was a lot of traffic on the way there. We had to park away from where the event was being held and take a shuttle bus to the beach party. There were so many tents and people on the beach; I didn't know where we would find a place to sit our things down and chill like everyone else. If I came again I knew we would have to come early to get a good spot. As we were walking around with our bags and beach towels, I ran into the guy that I had sex with in Puerto Rico. I almost walked right past him but he grabbed my arm.

"Hey Dontae. You are just going to walk right past me without saying hello? I thought we are better than that, considering the night we spent together in San Juan."

"Oh my goodness, are you following me?"

"As much as I would love to follow you around the country considering the night we had, the answer is no. I am on the Gay Black Pride board in Atlanta, and we get to check out all the prides around the country to promote Atlanta pride and see what things we can use to make our pride better."

"I was joking, I know you aren't following me, but anyway I am not paying attention, we just got to the beach and we are looking for somewhere to lay our towels and chill but it's so crowded and it looks like every piece of the beach is taken."

"Well, yeah you're right. We got here at seven a.m. this morning to pitch our tent and get a good place on the beach. We have plenty of room down near the beachfront and you and your friends are more than welcome to come down and chill with us."

"That sounds good – hey everyone, this is Omar, he said we can go down to where he and his friends are and get comfortable. Omar, this is David, who I think you met with me in Puerto Rico, and these are my friends from back home, Lonnie and Keith." Everyone shook Omar's hand as we walked down to where his friends were. They had a large tent where two other guys were laying inside drinking cocktails and eating fried chicken. Omar introduced us to his posse of friends and we dropped our things off and he made all four of us drinks. The two of his friends were in the tent smoking weed. I had not really been all that of a weed smoker, only trying it a couple of times in high school and undergrad. I liked drinking more; it seemed to relax me and lower my inhibition, I was a lot more outgoing after a few drinks.

Omar and I got reacquainted. He said he really enjoyed meeting me in Puerto Rico and had wished I had called him and kept in touch, but he felt since we ran into each other again we were meant to be more than just "pride fuck buddies" or a "one-night-stand." I explained to him that when I got back to Washington it was all business and no play due to the demands of my summer job. I also told him I was working at a law firm that didn't give me much time to do anything and when I did get home, all I wanted to do was sleep. He too was staying in the Westin and was hoping that I would come to his room again just like Puerto Rico. I didn't want to say no because I was too attracted to this man; he was fine. He was my height, but probably had me by about fifteen pounds of solid muscle. He was a cinnamon brown complexion with a bald head that looked real sexy on him. He said he used to model when he was younger and I could definitely see him in one of those black men calendars that Jemal and a lot of gay men and black women kept in their bathrooms. Omar was a nice guy but I felt he was too old for me, and the way he treated me made me feel like I was a young buck and not his equal.

I must admit that his sex was probably the best that I ever had. He worked my body so passionately that night in Puerto Rico, every stroke that went inside and out was amazing. He had me calling him "Papi" and neither one of us spoke a lick of Spanish. But I guess I had gotten so overcome by the language and the people, and Spanish was considered a romantic language that I let Omar have full control that night. Something I rarely did when I was just hooking up with someone. I also thought I would never be seeing him again so I had that what-the-hell attitude. Now that I had run into him again, I was sure he was expecting me to let him have his way again, and to be honest I didn't even know if I was in the mood for all that this trip. He had caught me off guard and at a vulnerable point in my life when I was feeling sad about Darrel abandoning our relationship. Even though I would still like closure with Darrel I had gotten used to the fact that we weren't together anymore. I no longer missed him or needed to be around him; he had become a distant memory, definitely one of life's heartbreaks, but something that I had overcome. It was true when they say: time heals all wounds, even the wounds of the heart, and unlike my first I didn't need another guy to make me feel special to get over the one I loved.

We ended up taking several pictures on the beach and I had way too much to drink by the time the beach party was over. I had my face in the sand, too drunk to stand up straight and get on the bus. Omar stood me up and walked me to his car and told my friends that he would make sure that I got back to the hotel safely. Although I was drunk and could barely function I could hear my friends in the background telling me to get it together and come back on the bus and then to the car with them. The liquor had me in a state of near-total incoherence and it felt nice to be taken care of like this by a strong man. My father was never really around to take care of me. Being as drunk as I was, I was kind of feeling bad that I had accomplished so much; I was able to move across the country, do well in school, and secure a good job that allowed me to take trips over the summer break; but I really didn't have a mother or father to call and let them know that life was going okay. All the accomplishments I had done and I didn't have anyone to share them with. It was true that too much alcohol can act as a downer.

Not even thinking because of my drunken stupor, I told them to leave and I would meet up with them later. It took Omar and his buddies about twenty minutes to gather their belongings and since they had come so early they were able to park close to the beach and not have to take the shuttle into the party area. When I got into the back seat one of Omar's friends was all in my ear, "Damn shawty you is sexy, you was drinking those drinks like they were kool-aid." I was too drunk to respond and my head was beginning to spin. While we were driving I told them to pull over because I needed to throw up. Before they could get the car to a complete stop I threw up on Omar's friend who was getting too fresh with me in the back seat. I didn't feel bad at all for throwing up on him because he was getting on my nerves. I was kind of embarrassed that I let myself get this intoxicated though.

I ended up passing out right after I threw up and I had woken up with Omar trying to get me to stand up so I could walk inside the hotel. "Damn baby, you really are fucked up. Are you going to be alright? You know I have my own suite so let's go back to my room so that you can get yourself together. Here is your cell phone it was on the floor on the backseat of the rental." I stumbled my way into the entrance of the Westin. There were a lot of dudes standing outside waiting on their cars to come out of valet, or just outside seeing who they could take back upstairs to their room. I didn't want to look like a total lush so I straightened up real quick when I saw a group a guys just staring at me.

I had been working out really hard this summer because the law firm had a gym in the building where I worked, and it was free for employees and interns so I took advantage of this opportunity. J.P. and Kenya had started telling me recently that I had lost a little weight and my waist looked smaller and my chest was poking out. I remembered Kenya saying, "Damn Dontae, you starting to look too good. One of these days I am going to have to show you what a real woman is working with." We both laughed and after that I started to notice that my clothes were fitting a little loosely and I was able to move forward a couple of holes on my belt buckle.

When the guys were staring at me, I immediately thought they could tell that I was drunk, because I had no shoes or shirt on. Then as we were passing the group of guys, Omar put his arms around my shoulder as if he was marking his territory. He then said, "I see you have been working out hard in the gym. I don't remember you having this much body, you got all the guys lusting after you out here, let me hurry up and get you up to my room." Then he laughed and held me tighter and I thought to myself that if I wasn't so fucked up, I would have moved away from his embrace. I knew what we did in Puerto Rico but to be honest it was really just a one-night-stand for me. I didn't think that I would ever run into this guy again, let alone be chilling with him and his friends. We had fun together and that was really all I wanted from him and it looked like he wanted some of this again. I think he was going to get what he wanted because he was very persistent. Plus as soon as we got to the room he started licking my nipples so sensually with his tongue and he had one of those oversized ones that I was sure he could lick his own nose. He had me thinking I just found my spot. I felt like I could cum by just him licking up and down and side to side, giving each nipple the same amount of attention, not wanting to neglect one for the other. My body was more sensitive because I had been drinking and smoking and the intensity heightened when he ran his long tongue down the nape of my back and inside the crevices of my buttocks. He was handling me like I was a morsel of his favorite pastry and he wanted to savor every moment. My thoughts and mind went blank when he forced his tongue in between my cheeks. I wanted to shiver in satisfaction, but the penetration was feeling so good I started to rock back and forth so that he could get deeper, and as his tongue inched its way through my tight muscle I couldn't help but moan, and the moaning didn't stop.

While he kept up with the motion of my rocking, and his tongue was sliding in and out I heard him rip open a condom and something else. As soon as the moisture of the lube touched my body it cooled me down a little bit. He then turned me on my back; parted my legs until they were dangling on his shoulders. I saw the black condom over his erect penis, while he got on his knees and rubbed his member back and forth between my cheeks very delicately trying to open me up. When he finally parted my ass enough for his member to slide all the way inside me he yelled, "Damn that shit feels good."

I concurred by saying, "You have no idea." Then as he swerved up and around and inside, my moaning turned into, "Take that shit, beat it up." I didn't know if he was turned on or off by it, all I knew was that he got deeper and deeper. When I woke up the next morning we were on the bathroom floor with towels underneath us, a sheet over us and I had the worst headache imaginable.

It was only five a.m. in the morning on Sunday and I had to be back at work the next day on Monday with bells on. Omar was still asleep on the floor next to me and he looked so peaceful. When I got up and went into the bathroom in the bedroom to get myself together to go to my room I noticed that we had fucked the suite up, everything that was on any type of flat surface was on the floor. There were no sheets or pillows on the bed and the shower was still running in the bedroom bathroom. All I could say was, damn, we must've fucked like porn stars last night.

I had twenty missed calls and they were all from David and Lonnie. I didn't feel like checking my messages so I just called Lonnie and asked where they were. "Hey, I am just waking up you know I was wasted last night."

"Yeah, everyone at the beach knows. We have been trying to reach you all night to see if you were okay. Damn, you should have at least let us know what room number you were in. Anyway, we are just leaving this after-hour spot at the Marriot that was wack and turned into a sex party, so we're about to go hit up Denny's up near the hotel. David met some guy at the club and just called me to tell him to meet him at Denny's."

"Okay, damn I cannot believe I missed the last night of partying in L.A. There must have been something in those drinks because I don't know what got over me."

"Wasn't nothing in those drinks but alcohol, it's just you was treating them like you was drinking water after a marathon."

"Whatever, I am hungry. Come get me from the hotel, I want to go to Denny's too."

"Where is Omar? He can drive you, can't he? David is already waiting on us."

"He is asleep and stop being shady and come pick me up, David don't want you."

"I will be there in ten minutes and be standing downstairs," Lonnie said and hung the phone up. I called myself trying to sneak out of the room and go back to my room and put some clothes on before I heard my name being called.

"Yo sexy, you about to roll out without even saying goodbye? The way I had you screaming my name last night I would have thought I could have gotten a goodbye kiss or something."

"No, it's not like that, it is just my friends have been calling me all night and I was about to go upstairs and change and go to Denny's with them. They just left the club." I felt like I was being held hostage. I finally realized what was wrong with him, he was a little too pressed. He was fine and could lay it down, but the sense of urgency and clinginess was kind of turning me off. I really didn't remember last night fully all I knew was when I walked I could feel it in my stance.

"Well I am hungry too, go to your room and put some clothes on and come back down and we will drive to meet up with your friends." I wanted to protest so bad but I didn't want to be mean. So I moped down to the room, called Lonnie and told him I would meet him at the Denny's, hopped in the shower and put some fresh clothes on. When I got back up to Omar's suite he grabbed me real hard and kissed me on the lips. I couldn't take it anymore; I needed to let him know that we were cool but not that cool. I was fucked up last night. That didn't mean we were lovers.

"Look, both times I have run into you we have had a good time. However, you're a little more affectionate than I am comfortable with and I don't want there to be a problem." Immediately after the statement came out my mouth I felt bad, because his smile turned into a frown and his brown eyes turned to sad puppy dog eyes.

"My bad Dontae. I thought you was feeling me like that, I didn't mean to cross the line."

"Man, it's okay. Maybe I am the one with the issues. I didn't grow up being all touchy-feely, so it just makes me uncomfortable. I feel like you are all over me and I am not used to that." I couldn't believe I shared that with him because this was really the first time I realized that affection was something that I didn't know how to accept. I always felt weird hugging people that I really didn't know all that well, or hugging people in general.

When I was in Seattle the white gay men liked to kiss you on your lips after saying hello, and I was definitely not into that. I guess that was why most people thought I was shady. And when I thought about it, Omar wasn't all that bad. Maybe since there was no real closure with Darrel, I wasn't able to accept anyone else in my life, I needed to get over the fact that maybe it was too good to be true and let the baggage go. I could tell that Omar was a good guy; I needed to ease up a little bit and stop being mean.

THE SUMMER WAS OVER and classes started in two days when I finally heard from Darrel. He asked me if I could meet him for coffee on U Street and that he wanted to explain everything to me. I was reluctant in meeting because I had finally gotten over the fact that I probably would never see or hear from him again, and I was fine with that. Omar and I had been talking on the phone on a regular basis and I had plans to go to Atlanta for Labor Day weekend to see him and spend some time. During the weeks following my trip to L.A., I had become very fond of Omar. It turned out that we had a lot in common as far as how we were raised and it felt good to have someone I could talk to who could relate to me.

When I arrived at the small coffee shop, Darrel was seated at a table in the back, where nobody was located. I was sure he picked this location strategically so we could have privacy and talk. He looked real good I must admit, and when he smiled at me and said hello all my feelings came back to surface.

"I almost thought that you would stand me up, and I guess I couldn't blame you if you did. I have been waiting on you for over a half hour." He motioned for me to sit down.

"No, I was running late I had to pick Jemal up from the airport and drop him off at the apartment, and not to mention it took forever to find a parking spot."

"Well, you are here now, and I ordered you an ice frappuccino. It's really good to see you and I know you must hate me right now, but after my father passed I was in a state of shock and didn't know how to cope. I made a rash decision and eloped with my high school sweetheart and bought a house in Capitol Heights, and she is now three months pregnant."

I couldn't believe all this happened in such a short period of time. Darrel had been busy. Married? I had to take a deep breath because I couldn't believe I just heard him say he was married and expecting a child.

"So you're married now and to think I came down here thinking you were going to try and get back together with me, and tell me how much you missed me and needed time to get over your father's death. I would have never imagined you would be dropping this bomb. I didn't even know you were still interested in women."

"Well you're not totally wrong, I do miss you like crazy and I am miserable in this situation. I know it is selfish to ask you this but I was hoping that we could start seeing each other again?"

As soon as he said that, I spit the coffee that I had just drank out my mouth, trying not to laugh in his face. "Darrel, although I wish you would have allowed me to help you through your tragedy so we could still be together now. The fact that you didn't allow me to let's me know that you didn't love me like I thought you did. Too much time has gone by and I have moved on, plus I don't think you are in a situation to be seeing me or anyone at the moment."

"I know how you must feel, and I don't know how things will work out if you did decide to start seeing me again. I know I don't want to leave my wife while she is pregnant but I thought if I started seeing you again then I wouldn't always be so miserable."

As this conversation was progressing I was thinking to myself he must have bumped his head if he thought I would agree to those terms. I was getting kind of agitated by the whole ordeal and was ready to end the conversation at this point before I felt totally disrespected. "Darrel, it was good seeing you, but I have another engagement that I need to attend tonight. If you ever need to talk you have my number, but too much has happened and I only want to be friends."

I started to get up and walk out the coffee shop, and when I looked back hoping this would be the last time I saw Darrel again, he looked very pitiful and said, "Dontae, I really need you right now, don't walk out on me." He was in tears by this time, but that was just what I did – I walked out. I knew Darrel felt hurt right now, but I had been going through this for several months wondering what he was doing, and if he was okay. He hurt me and I couldn't allow him to do it again and this time he was asking me to participate in the process. I wasn't having it, as much as I wanted to leave the shop with him and hold him in my arms, and kiss him and tell him everything was going to be okay. I knew that there was no way given the current circumstances it would ever be okay.

CHAPTER 9

J.P.

I loved the part of the Fall when it was not too cold and too hot. The leaves turned yellow and orange and you could feel the breeze on your skin. That always relaxed me. The summer was over so this meant it was time for planning for the holiday season and the upcoming New Year. Since the year was almost over I could reflect on all the things that had occurred and develop an adequate game plan on improving my state of being. I decided to take a break from law school for the time being. I finished my first year on a good note. I ended up doing well the last semester, which balanced out my first-semester grades, so I was now in good standing. I decided after working in the law firm this summer that right now singing was my number-one priority.

The week before classes were to begin, I had auditioned for American Idol and made it to Hollywood week, which would begin in November. I was so excited when all three judges unanimously said they loved my voice and they thought I was one of the best singers that they had heard in a while. I was in tears when I walked out of the audition room into the arms of Dontae and Kenya. They both hugged me and said they had no doubt that I would make it to the next round and they would be surprised if I didn't make it to the finals. I wasn't that confident because I watched the show before, and sometimes the people I thought had the best voices did not make it. So I planned to just do my best and hoped that this would be a door-opener for me.

I knew my father knew all three of the judges personally from conversations we had. He even declined an opportunity to be one of the guest judges one year when they had celebrity judges on every week. So as soon as I walked out of the convention center where the auditions were being held with my yellow ticket to Hollywood, I called daddy to tell him the good news. I was certain that he would have been a little disappointed that I didn't seek his advice or include him in the process, but this was something that I needed to do for me. I wanted to do this on my own, succeed or fail. I made it a point to stay far under the radar given who my father was. I didn't want to be seen as another Paris Hilton or heiress given the spotlight because of who their parents were. When the phone rang daddy answered on the first ring. "Hey baby girl, how are you doing? You staying cool? I am sure the weather is crazy down there as it is up here. Veronica and I are burning up!"

"I am doing great, daddy, I called you with some good news."

"What news, baby?"

"Hold up daddy I was just about to tell you," I laughed. He was already excited and didn't even know what was going on with me. Well you know that show American Idol that you were about to go on? Anyway I just made it to the Hollywood week. I am leaving the D.C. convention center now, with Dontae and Kenya. We are about to go somewhere and celebrate, but I had to call you and tell you."

"This is very shocking to hear. I always knew you had taken after your mother with having a great voice, but I thought singing was the last thing you wanted to do. I always thought you were more focused on school and getting a good education."

"Well yeah, daddy, there are a lot of things that have changed about me since I moved to D.C. When you come down next week, I will explain everything to you. Now I have to go because Kenya and Dontae want to go celebrate."

"Alright, baby, if this is what you really want to do, I look forward to seeing you on the show. Is there anything you want me to do? You know I know a lot people connected with that show."

"No daddy that is the last thing I want you to do is go pulling strings for me. I want to make it because the judges and America think I can really sing, okay?"

"Okay baby, I was just checking. You know how overprotective I am over you."

"I know daddy, but there are some things I can do on my own but I love you and I will call you later."

"Love you too, bye baby." I didn't think he would ever let me get off the phone. I knew I had just dropped a bomb and he already wanted to call in the favors.

Since school was going to start that following week, I withdrew, and I had been helping Kenya start her business, volunteering at the day school at Metropolitan Baptist church where I am a proud member, and working in the music department with two choirs. Daddy lent Kenya the seed money to pay for a full year of office space in a new building in the downtown business district and he gave her some old office furniture that his company had in storage after they remodeled.

Things were starting to fall into place with her plan. She initially went to the bank to ask for a loan, and they turned her down because she didn't have any collateral. She wanted to look for grants and apply for a business loan from the district, but when I told daddy about her business plan he had his lawyers take a look at it, and less then twenty-four hours he wrote her a check. Since I had a lot of time on my hands waiting for Hollywood week to begin I served as Kenya's personal assistant while she got her business off the ground. She couldn't afford to hire Elaine her old assistant yet.

My duties mainly consisted of answering phone calls, scheduling meetings and making sure that the telecommunication needs for the office were met, as far as getting phone lines and hooking up the Internet. So my days started off with opening up the office around seven-thirty in the morning, then I left around eleven to go to the day school and work with the little kids I have grown to love. Then I leave around two in the afternoon and close the office around five-thirty. Kenya was still in school; she planned to have her masters at the end of this semester so she could focus all her time on the business. Being able to help her worked out very well with her schedule and also gave me something to do.

Ever since Kurt called me back in December, we had been seeing each other on a regular basis. Even though he resided in Miami, he spent every chance he got in D.C. with me. Even though his high school sweetheart, Cherry, tricked him into thinking that her third son was his, he still went to go visit her and his kids in Philly and dropped by to see me. I drove up there with him in the beginning of the summer. We took the kids to Six Flags Great Adventure in New Jersey and had a blast. I could tell Kurt didn't mind that Cherry's other son wasn't his; he never left the little boy out when he came to pick up his biological kids. I too wanted kids, and at the rate we were going – I hoped, I didn't jinx myself by saying this – but one day he was the father of my biological kids and my adopted kids.

Kurt was very supportive when I made it to the second round of American Idol. He and I celebrated by going to Hawaii and having a good time the week I decided I would withdraw from classes. Kurt was a romantic lover; he catered to my every need and he made me feel special. It didn't take any time for him to make me forget that I was ever in love with Ronnie.

I had spoken to Ronnie a few times since our breakup. He called to see if I wanted to perform a couple of times. I declined because I really didn't want to relive the past, and I knew even though Ronnie didn't want to be with me romantically, we had tremendous sexual chemistry and I didn't want that to confuse my feelings. The only singing I had been doing publicly was for the Lord and I enjoyed it as much as performing on stage with the band. Daddy now wanted me to get a vocal coach and start practicing different songs from different genres so that I could be prepared for the whole American Idol process. I told him I didn't need a stage father while I went through the process. I did plan on practicing different types of music so I wouldn't be caught off-guard when I entered the competition. I had to be firm that I would be doing everything on my own.

I was really excited and antsy about Hollywood week. Of course I wanted to make it all the way, but I kept telling myself I needed to take it one step at a time. It was nerve-wrecking waiting for the time to come. When you watch it on TV everything just happened so fast, so I had know idea of the actual waiting process that was involved. When I auditioned back in August, D.C. was the first city on the judges' tour list and they still had several other cities to go to before they picked all the contestants that would be headed to Hollywood. My waiting period was therefore a lot longer than some had and it was hard to deal with. I wanted to get the show on the road and show America what I was working with.

TODAY WAS HALLOWEEN AND KURT and I planned on driving to King's Dominion, the theme park about an hour and a half away, right outside Richmond. The park was usually closed for the fall and winter because of the weather but opened up around Halloween for their haunted attractions. Kurt was a kid at heart and I enjoyed watching him enjoy himself; it made me feel like a kid again. Since it was just me and my mom most of the time I really didn't get to do a lot of the stuff normal kids did, unless it was my weekend with daddy and even then he wasn't into roller coasters, jet skiing or most of the things Kurt did as a kid.

Dating a professional basketball player kept me somewhat in the limelight. I had seen my picture in a couple of newspapers and magazines while out with Kurt. Of course nobody knew who I was so my name was never printed, but some of my sorority sisters called me and said they saw me in Vibe or their local newspaper. And Kurt didn't make it any better, walking around any and everywhere like he was common folk. He loved to sign autographs too; I cannot tell you how many movies, plays and events we were late to because he had a line of autographs to sign. I kind of liked the attention, though, and if I ever made it famous I think I would be the same way.

Kurt came from a loving home having grown up in Philly. When he made it pro he moved his family to the suburbs outside of Philly in South Jersey. They lived in a nice gated community with a pool in the backyard, a country club and a golf course located around the community. I didn't play too much golf, but my father did and he always said he was going to teach me one day. For some reason I had no interest in learning how to play golf, though, so I always made myself unavailable.

Kurt took me to his parents' home one day when we were up in Philly visiting the kids. I was kind of reluctant because I really didn't know how to react around a traditional family. Every family situation I had ever encountered had been dysfunctional, but his mother Stella made me feel comfortable. I could see where he got his height from because Stella was over six feet tall and his father was only five-seven. You could tell she ruled her home; she had a very dominant personality. His father was very soft-spoken and didn't say very much, and it appeared that he followed Stella around the house or wherever she was going. After I spent the afternoon with Stella, she took me into their sunroom and told me that she was glad that her son had finally met a nice girl who had gone to college and wasn't from the block. She confessed that she was kind of worried that he wouldn't be able to get over his high school sweet heart, Cherry, who she despised because of what she had put their family through. Listening to his mother I could really tell that she loved her son and wanted the best for him. I gave her my cell phone number and she had called to check on me a couple of times since I met her, which I thought was nice. Kurt had mentioned to her that my mother had passed. It felt good to talk to an older-women about what I was going through.

Kurt and I had a ball on Halloween night. We ended up going to eat at a soul food restaurant and stayed in a nearby Hilton Hotel for the night. We both drank way too much and neither wanted to drive the two hours back to my apartment in D.C. This was the beginning of the basketball season for him and he was scheduled for practice the next day in Miami because there was a home game the following day. He really didn't want to travel to D.C. so close to his opening game. But when I told him that I couldn't make it to Miami until the day of his game because I had to work at the school with the kids he decided that he would make the trip to spend the day with me. It was great to know that he wanted to spend so much time with me; at first I didn't think that a long distance relationship could work, but that died when his team lost in the semifinals last season. It was almost as if he moved in with me over the summer months. When I got home from my internship he either had dinner ready or told me to get dressed so that we could go out on the town. During the two summer holidays Memorial Day and the Fourth of July, we spent our time at his place out in Miami.

The first time going back to his place after what happened while I was on spring break kind of made me feel uneasy. However, after making sweet passionate love in every nook and cranny of the mansion the first night there I was more than comfortable, and was able to almost erase the bad memories. I always asked him if he felt weird when he was in D.C. staying in my small apartment considering he owned and lived in a mansion. Of course he said he enjoyed it and as long as I was there with him he would be able to stay anywhere. I knew when I left his home and went back to my own place I missed his large whirlpool Jacuzzi tub where I would sit and take bubble baths or he and I would lay side by side talking about our lifelong goals. What would he do once I became a famous singer and I was traveling as much as he was and we wouldn't have these times together? He would always get sad and tell me that playing basketball you would get used to the schedule and the routine of the season, but as a pop star you didn't have any seasons. You would be expected to be out during the whole year if you were that popular.

I reassured him that I would be spending as much time with him as possible, and I also hinted around about how he could assure that it would happen – marriage, of course. He always got shy when I talked about weddings and engagement rings. He did confess to me that I would be the perfect woman for him to marry during Labor Day when we were in Spain. We were in Spain because a college teammate of his was playing in the European Basketball League finals. I didn't know if it was because Spain was so romantic or it was it all the champagne we had that night at the club, but it was also the first time he said he loved me and couldn't imagine his life without me. I had been in love with Kurt for several months before he acknowledged it, but I guess I still carried some negative baggage from my relationship with Ronnie so I never admitted to him that I loved him before that night. I didn't want to assume something that wasn't mutual, so it was really refreshing hearing the words come out his mouth. I already knew for a man, especially a strong black man that those words were hard to come by.

Things finally seemed to be in my favor and I was glad about it. Daddy was meeting me in Miami for Kurt's opening game, not because he liked the Heat, but because they were playing the New York Nicks, daddy's favorite team. This would give him an excuse to check up on his only daughter and to spend sometime with Kurt. He and Kurt had hit it off instantly when they met. I could tell daddy always wanted a son and he treated Kurt like he was his new son. He was always giving him advice on his game, finances and me for that matter. I had to interfere when it came to giving advice on me; that was getting a little too involved and he was my dad, not Kurt's. Daddy and I would both be staying at Kurt's place. At first Daddy tried to make reservations at a hotel, but Kurt wouldn't allow it. Veronica had taken her mother to the South to visit their relatives so he would be traveling alone and so was I. I tried convincing Dontae to come down and miss a few classes, but he was so dedicated to being at the top of his program he declined my invitation. Kenya also declined and said that she had too much schoolwork and had some very important presentations that she needed to prepare to give for some potential business opportunity.

I will say Kenya had really been working nonstop to ensure that her business had taken off. She had gotten on the 8(a) minority contractor list for the government to provide temporary and long-term work assignments. She met with several of the larger businesses in the D.C. metropolitan area and informed them of her services and the need to employ the many D.C. minority residents who were finding it hard to find adequate jobs; informing them that many residents were finding it difficult to survive due to the increased cost of living in the area. Kenya mentioned that the D.C. area was beginning to become unaffordable for its residents because of the rapidly growing housing market. Most of the current jobs on the market required higher skills than African-Americans traditionally had acquired. Many people around the country or from other countries were moving to Washington taking up these jobs. So Kenya was not only working with the government and employers to hire minority applicants, she was also providing classes and workshops to prepare her talent for these jobs. She realized that she wasn't capable of fixing the problem in its entirety but providing competitive incomes for at least some families would allow some folks to prosper, and that was all that mattered.

Coming from poverty herself, Kenya could really relate to the people that her company was employing. She was such a success story and I was proud to know someone who was so selfless that she wanted to dedicate her life and her well-being into making sure others could live a better life. It was why I had been there from the beginning taking flyers to get printed, answering phone calls, setting up appointments and whatever it was that she needed to make sure this operation worked.

When I arrived at the Miami International Airport, I had to take a cab to the mansion because Kurt was with his team getting ready for the opening game. He gave me a set of keys when I was down here last. Daddy's flight didn't come in for another two hours. He said he would rent a car and meet me at American Airlines Arena to watch the game.

As soon as I got my luggage from baggage claim and went to ground transportation to pick up a cab, I ran into Cordel. I froze as soon as I saw his face; I was too startled to run in the other direction and I was ten feet away from where he was. He noticed me the same time I had noticed him. I couldn't pick up my feet and move and I felt like I was going to pee on myself. I knew that nothing could happen to me in front of all these people, but I was still terrified of this man and I just thought to myself that I should've had this fool locked up so I wouldn't have to run into his ass again. Then before I could gain my composure I heard him calling my name.

"J.P., J.P.... I have been wanting to run into you or at least get in touch with you for a while now," Cordel said as he walked up to me. I didn't know what he wanted to talk to me about and I sure as hell didn't want to hear what this slime ball had to say to me. So I got enough nerve and tried to walk out the airport double doors before he grabbed me and turned me back around. "Look J.P., I have changed. I was so drunk and coked out that night I attacked you at the party, I barely remember it. Probably the only reason why I do remember it is because I lost the most significant person in my life over what happen, and that was Kenya. I had no right to force myself on you the way I did, for so many reasons. You didn't know and neither did Kenya, but that weekend I had just found out that I was dropped from the Atlanta Falcons for showing up positive for steroids, marijuana, cocaine and amphetamines. I heard the news when I was in California planning my wedding with Kenya and my agent immediately flew me to Miami for an underground meeting with the owner and the head coach with the Miami Dolphins, so I could get a hush transfer. They made me go into rehab before I could even sign the contract and play for the team. I have been sober for over two years now, I have a therapist that I see on a regular basis to help me handle my anger issues and I am a devoted minister at a church right here in Miami talking to young men and women about overcoming substance abuse and crime. I really am sorry for my actions and I hope you know that I would never do anything like that again in my life. I hope you forgive me and I hope you can tell Kenya that I never meant to hurt her and I hope she forgives me too."

By the time he finished what he had to say, I was in tears, and I reached over to him and gave him a big hug. I could see in his eyes that he was hurting and that he was really sorry for what he had done. I had been through a lot since the incident and I was not holding any grudges towards this man, especially since he had repented to God. I knew if God forgave him so should I. I whispered in his ear while still holding him tight, "I appreciate you being man enough to admit you made a mistake and rectify it. Up until today the violation has been something that has haunted me ever since that day. Now that I know what state of mind you were in, I feel relieved to know that it was nothing that I did wrong in the situation. As much as I wanted to be healed emotionally and mentally, it's hard for a victim not to ask themselves what they did wrong, what could they have done to prevent the situation from occurring. Most of us never have this opportunity to know that there are forces bigger than them that allow bad things to occur. It was good seeing you and I hope you enjoy your weekend." I released the embrace between the two of us and headed out to get in my cab.

When I arrived at the mansion I had about three hours before it would be time for me to head to the game. I ate at the airport waiting on my flight to Miami and I wasn't hungry, so I decided I would take a swim in Kurt's Olympic-size pool. Swimming always relaxed me and it was good exercise. I was told in gym class growing up that swimming worked every muscle in your body. The weather was around 85 degrees, but it felt like it was 90 and it was 50 degrees back in D.C., so I wanted to take advantage of the nice weather as well.

When I got finished showering I blew-dry my hair, slicked it back and curled the back and wore my jersey skirt I had made with Kurt's last name and number on the back. I had also put on a fitted hat he bought for me a couple of months ago. I probably was doing too much, but I wanted him to know that I was proud of him and I was his girl. I also knew daddy was gong to be sporting his Nicks attire so I wanted to balance him out and not have Kurt thinking I was a traitor.

The game ended in overtime with Miami winning their home opening 76-69. This was a really good way to start the season, I thought to myself, as I waited for Kurt outside the stadium. Daddy had a few friends that he wanted to catch up with for drinks and he and Kurt and I planned on driving to Boca Raton in the morning so Daddy could look at some property that he wanted to buy. Kurt and I celebrated together and of course it consisted of going to an after-party at a few clubs and since the team won the players were treated like royalty. It always amazed me at how so many girls threw themselves on professional athletes. Many of the girls that I associated with in D.C. since I'd been dating Kurt would ask me how to snag a ball player. I really didn't have any advice for them because to be honest snagging a ball player wasn't really my intent. A lot of them thought I was full of shit when I told them that, but I really didn't think there was a guide book out there. What I had noticed was that most of the time the women who were searching and looking for these men rarely found them. If they did it was nothing more than a hook-up. The wives and the girlfriends that I had met since dating Kurt had all told me they either met their man in college or high school. So I would say to all the ladies trying to snag a ball player that their best bet would be to enroll their daughters in colleges and high schools where the best players were balling and try to live vicariously through them.

THE DAY I HAD BEEN WAITING for was tomorrow: I would board my flight to Hollywood, California to continue my quest in becoming the next American Idol. Kurt had a game in Dallas tonight, so he wasn't here to wish me off, but daddy, Kenya, Dontae and I all had dinner together to wish me off. Daddy almost begged me to allow him to come with me so he could be there for support and I told him that I would be fine. Honestly the only person who I wished could be there with me holding my hand was Kurt, but he was too busy with his basketball season, and plus it would be too much publicity if he were there with me. I packed for a week, hoping that I would last the whole week. The American Idol producers sent me a plane ticket to Hollywood and had transportation set up for me from the airport to the hotel.

When I got to L.A., there were about twenty people who had arrived around the same time as I did and we all took a charter bus to the hotel. They had us staying in the Quality Inn near the airport and there were three to a room. When I got there both my roommates were already in the room and they had picked the areas where they would be sleeping during the week, which left me on the pullout sofa. I really didn't mind, I was just happy to be here. The two girls introduced themselves as Sarah and Monica. Sarah was twenty-two and from Montana, she said she auditioned in Portland. She was a cocktail waitress and loved singing country music. She had dishwater blond hair that she wore pulled back in a ponytail. She had that small-town appeal that I had seen from many contestants who were on American Idol from previous seasons. Her looks were above-average and she had a real nice figure. The only problem that I saw with her physical appearance was that she had a lot of crowding in her bottom teeth. They kind of overlapped each other. She tried to hide it by only showing her top row of teeth which were in a straight perfect row. Monica on the other hand was the exact opposite of Sarah. She was a larger-framed girl, not overweight, but big-boned. If I would guess she was about a size ten. She dressed in all black, and wore her jet-black hair in a short spiked cut. She had on purple lipstick, real dark eyeshadow and her nails and toes were painted black. I assumed by the way she looked she was the resident Rocker. Monica was born and raised in New York City and said she had just turned down an off-Broadway starring role in the musical "Hair Spray" to come to Hollywood.

The girls seemed pretty cool: both were just as excited as I was to be in Hollywood, and Monica confessed that she had made it to Hollywood last year and wasn't picked for the semi-finals. She said she knew that this was her time to make it all the way. She said she spent the last year taking vocal lessons and auditioning for any and everything that came her way. Since this was Sarah and my first time, we looked at Monica as kind of like an elder, someone to help us through the process; we felt like we had insider knowledge listening to the stories she told about last year's Hollywood week.

We went to bed early because we had a note in our room saying that we needed to be ready to leave at six a.m. so that we could catch the shuttle to start the first day. There was only one bathroom in the hotel room so I got up first so I wouldn't be late. Since I would be on camera I made sure I got a fresh relaxer and wrap right before I came to Hollywood, so my auburn locks would be flowing beautifully as I walked off and on the stage. I slept with a scarf on my head so I didn't have to do too much to my do. When I finished getting ready I had about forty-five minutes before the shuttle left and my two roommates still weren't out of bed. So I took it upon myself to play mother and make sure they were up in time to make the shuttle and not be eliminated from the competition before it even began. They both jumped up and panicked when they saw that I was completely dressed and ready to go. I reassured them that I couldn't really sleep, and I had woken up way too early. I wanted to be out of their way so they would have plenty of time to dress and make the shuttle. After the girls started getting ready I told them I would get out of their way and meet them downstairs in the lobby.

When I got to the lobby I noticed that I wasn't the only one who couldn't sleep the night before or who wanted to be early. There were about thirty people of all different sizes, colors and styles in the lobby waiting for the shuttle buses to arrive and take us to the Orpheum Theater where we would see the judges again. We all boarded the buses and headed to the theater and were told to sit in the audience. The program started with one of the producers by the name of Steven saying that we would be grouped in groups of three and we would have twenty songs to choose from the nineteen sixties and we would meet here tomorrow in front of the judges to perform the songs, and there would be a cut from 250 down to 175.

Everything after that first day went so fast it was a blur. All I remembered was I had made it through the entire week. The last day in the hotel room it was just me and Monica. Sarah had been eliminated on Wednesday and it was now Friday and it was down to thirty-five of us for only twenty-four spots. We had individual interviews with Paula, Randy and Simon where they would let us know individually if we made the live performances. I had used my mother's maiden name when I entered the competition and the producers had asked a lot of questions about my family. They wanted to focus on my mother's suicide and that was really hard for me to deal with and they had licensed psychologists on-site to help the folks with troubled past deal with it after the prying questions. I tried my best to keep my composure so that I could make it through the competition without breaking down. This was the first time I really had to deal with this tragedy in my life and tell my story to strangers. For years I had just blocked it out of my thoughts and kept it moving. Now I had to deal with it and they said that if I got further in the competition that it would be something that they would highlight so America could get to know me. They said it was my story and every contestant had to have one. Since I was over eighteen, I was able to sign the releases on my own and I really wanted to move forward so I went on ahead and signed the contract so I could move forward in the competition.

Luckily they weren't able to trace me back to my father, and I found that very surprising. When I told daddy what I had done, not using his last name and using Ma's maiden name, he was kind of disappointed but he understood that I was trying to make my own distinction in the world. I also told him that Ma's last name "popped," and it was more of a stage name. Vanderbilt sounded important and I thought many people would recognize it and not forget me. Peele just sounded too plain and there was already a famous actress by that name anyway, so by using this name I would be original.

I was probably the twelfth contestant to be called upstairs to meet with the judges and the guy that went before me had gotten bad news that he wasn't making it to the live semifinals, so I was extra nervous as I rode the elevator to the meeting room. When I got to the elevator and walked into the room the three judges were about twenty steps at the end of the room and they were staring at me with a stern look. I could not tell whether I made it or I was going home. There was one chair in the middle of the desk where they were sitting and they pointed for me to sit down when I got close enough to hear them.

"Jennifer Vanderbilt, how has your week been in Hollywood?" Randy Jackson asked me.

"I have enjoyed every minute and it is such an honor to have made it this far, thank you very much for choosing me."

"You're welcome," all the judges said in unison.

"Well, I am sure you want to know whether you made it or if you are going home, so let's get right to it," Simon said. "Randy."

"Yes!"

"Paula?"

"I just want to tell you that you have a beautiful voice and I cannot wait for America to get to know Jennifer. Yes!"

"Well, there you have it, and it really doesn't matter what I think. You have made it to the next round, we will be seeing you soon." Simon finished.

I was elated to hear the news and I couldn't believe it, I made it onto American Idol. I have watched the show faithfully and I would have never thought that I would be on the show myself. I ran out the room and pinched myself to make sure I wasn't dreaming and I was still on the top floor of the Orpheum Theater. Tears started coming down my eyes as one of the producers handed me the pass to the next round. When I got back down to the waiting room Monica was waiting for the news. She had yet to meet with the judges to see if she had made it to the next round. I whispered in her ear that I made it and she started screaming for me and then everyone who had made it and was still there and the contestants who were still waiting came up to me and hugged me and gave their congratulations. I promised Monica I would wait until she found out if she had made it too. I hoped she did because we had gotten close and I knew it would break her heart if she didn't make it. Plus it would give me an ally in the competition when everyone was hoping that you would be the next to get kicked off so they didn't have to leave.

I kind of feel bad for some of the contestants that didn't make it because they had left jobs, school, family and left bills unpaid to try out for their dream and didn't make it. However, Monica broke it down for me when Sarah left: that this was an opportunity of a lifetime, and if you made a sacrifice that you couldn't live with if you didn't make it then you shouldn't have entered the competition. I liked Monica for this. She reminded me of my mother, she said things that people didn't want to hear. That is why when we filled out our questionnaires and there was a question as to what judge was your favorite she picked Simon, because of his honesty. I on the other hand picked Paula because I felt like she was a true "pop star." She knew what it was like out there selling records, touring and developing a fan base.

I waited another hour with Monica before she was told that she had made it to the next round. We both took a cab to the hotel to collect our things because the next shuttle wasn't leaving for another hour. We both wanted to head back home as soon as possible so that we could be with our families and friends who we missed dearly. This week was emotionally draining and I we both felt like we didn't have any energy left to stay in Hollywood. The top-twenty-four round didn't begin for another six weeks and we both had our passes to come back, so we got out as fast as we could.

I flew to New York City so I could be with daddy and Veronica and they both greeted me at the airport with open arms. When we got into daddy's car, Kurt was seated in the backseat with a bouquet of roses and a black velvet jewelry box. Daddy and Veronica said they had car service waiting for them and let us take his car and his driver away from the airport. I was too excited to even understand what was going on, but when Kurt kissed me I knew what he was about to say next.

"Baby I am so proud that you made it to the next level, I was on the road rooting and praying for you. You see this box that I have in my hands? I have been wanting to give this to your for months I was just waiting for the right moment." He opened it up and there laid a seven carat diamond engagement ring. "Jennifer Elizabeth Peel, will you marry me and be my wife for the rest of our lives?"

"Yes, Kurt, I thought you would never ask. Being married to you would be better than winning American Idol. You have been such a great friend and I love you more than you know."

"J.P., you are my American Idol, and you are my world, I couldn't imagine spending my life without you and I am so glad that you said yes, because with everything that has been going on with your career, I wasn't sure that you were ready."

"I am ready baby. I am so ready to be 'Mrs.' Kurt Livingston."

CHAPTER 10

Dontae

The summer was about to begin and I had one more year left of law school and I was excited that I was still at the top of the class. Not the very top, but close enough that the law firm where I worked at last summer extended the same offer with a larger salary and they had already talked about me coming aboard as an associate when I graduated next year. The only problem with that was that I would be working in D.C. Since Omar and I had gotten real close and the long-distance relationship was killing me I was really considering a firm in Atlanta. I had spent all the extra money I had driving or flying to see him as much as I could since Labor Day of last year. Since he was already established, owned his own home and had a lot of business contacts down there it really didn't make sense for him to move up here. I didn't have any family in D.C so it made more sense for me to move down there.

I had never thought I would be the one to move from city to city for a man, but this really felt right and Omar had really grown on me in a way that nobody ever had. It was lonely being in D.C. without him and every time I left Atlanta or he would leave D.C., I found myself wishing that we could spend more time together. It kind of scared me how much I liked him and how jealous I got sometimes. I didn't know I had it in me to be so jealous, but they say love made you crazy. I had almost gotten into a fight in a club in Atlanta when I saw this guy touching and grabbing on Omar right in front of me. He wasn't doing anything about it. I couldn't believe how angry I was; luckily Omar was promoting the party so I wasn't put out, but I made a huge scene and the DJ stopped playing the music and they turned on the lights. Even though I wasn't put out, I wanted to leave immediately but we had to stay until the end. Omar still had to count all the money and pay everyone. When we had finally left the club well past six in the morning we went for breakfast and Omar explained to me that he was somewhat of a celebrity in Atlanta and a lot of guys flirted with him while he worked. He said it was part of the territory and he wanted people to continue to patronize his parties so he did a little flirting, but that was it.

I had a really hard time getting past the constant attention that he received. I didn't mind folks saying hello and being cordial but some of the guys took it way too far. I had been coming down here for several months so I knew most people knew he was dating me, so I found it outright disrespectful for dudes to be groping all up on what was mine.

After the scene I had caused I kept playing in my mind what he was doing while I was in D.C. and he was in Atlanta alone, probably lonely and throwing parties with all these guys throwing themselves on him. I was hoping that he was thinking about me and not being overcome by temptation. I knew I had been out on several occasions with David and some of the finest men had tried to holler at me, but I always remembered what I had with Omar and blocked every negative thought that would jeopardize my relationship.

The ultimate temptation came when I ran into Darrel at the library. He had come over to the table where I was studying and stood beside me until I looked up. I could feel someone near me, but I was so engrossed in my schoolwork that I didn't pay it any mind until I finished the chapter that I was reading. When I looked up he was right there standing beside me. He still looked good and when I looked into his eyes all the emotions that I thought were gone rushed right back to my heart like a tidal wave (there was something about this dude that made him hard for me to shake). Since there were people around studying we didn't say much but hello and how were things going. He said things hadn't changed he was still miserable, but he was a father now and that he loved his daughter. As soon as he said that reality had set back in and I ended the conversation immediately. I changed the subject and let him know that had so much studying to catch up on and needed to get back to it. I had just gotten back from Atlanta and didn't get any schoolwork done because Omar had kept me pretty busy doing other things.

Darrel had called and text me for months after seeing him in the library. He begged to see me. I had several voice mail messages saying the same thing, "I need you in my arms again, please don't walk out of my life, be there for me and I promise I will always be there for you." I didn't believe anything he had to say at this point. He had already made his choice so he needed to live with it, and leave me alone. He had a family and I knew that came first and I wasn't going to create an ugly situation for myself or him.

One rainy Saturday I didn't have anything to do. It was too ugly to go anywhere to pass the time, there was nothing on television and I was missing Omar so much. Jemal had been dating someone new and spent most of his free time at his new friends place out in Potomac. I was cramped in the apartment, alone, lonely and horny. Out of nowhere Darrel showed up on my doorstep unannounced. Since I was home alone and not expecting anyone I didn't know who was knocking at the door. When I looked through the peephole at first I didn't know who it was, but my eyes came into focus and I couldn't believe it was Darrel.

I didn't know why I let him in, but I did and I regretted it the minute I opened up the door. Darrel immediately grabbed me, holding me so tight I could barely breathe, and he wouldn't release me. The hug felt so good and I missed him so much; we really did have some good times together. But after the hug I completely forgot that I was dating someone and invited Darrel to sit down on the couch. Before I knew it he was undressing me, lifting my shirt off my chest and pulling down my shorts. Next thing I knew he had my rock hard member in his mouth and he was sucking it up and down like a lollipop. I knew I should have stopped what was going on but the sensation was feeling too good that I released right in his mouth. After I did there was an awkward moment of silence before he started crying and telling me that he needed me back in his life. He said he would do whatever it would take to get our relationship back—even if it meant leaving his wife.

I consoled him and allowed him to commiserate until we both passed out. When I woke up the next day he was gone. The phone calls continued along with the constant text messages, and finally I changed my number because I couldn't deal with the drama any longer. I also didn't want to mess up what I had with Omar and things were going good with us and that mattered to me the most. I felt guilty a couple of days after and I decided that I wouldn't tell Omar what happened, but I did promise myself that it would never happen again.

DURING MEMORIAL DAY I decided to stay in D.C. and Omar and his friends were going to come up. J.P. was in California pursuing her singing career on American Idol; she didn't win the competition, unfortunately, but she did make it to the final four. The season finale of the show was on Wednesday therefore Kenya and I were flying to L.A. to support our girl, while she closed the show for the season along with the rest of the final twelve contestants. She would be touring all summer long across the country and decided to turn over her apartment to me. Jemal decided he would be moving in with his boyfriend so everything worked out. I would finally have my own place and it was bittersweet. Jemal and I had gotten really close as roommates. It kind of started off rocky but we were able to get over our differences and learn to respect one another and live harmoniously. I would miss our late night talks, his home-cooked meals and the trips to the mall that we usually did on Saturdays. Well those didn't really have to stop but I had learned with past friends, there was usually that "out of sight/out of mind" thing that kicked in after a couple of weeks. It was sad to think that I probably wouldn't be seeing him all that much, but I doubt that we had enough stuff to keep us as close as we were. We were close because we were roommates and we were forced to see each other. I would just have to wait and see how things turned out, but I wished him all the best in his new relationship.

KENYA AND I HAD A BALL IN L.A. we had dinner with J.P., her father and Kurt. Other than the dinner we didn't really get to spend that much time with J.P., because she had a lot of rehearsals and practicing for the finale and her summer tour. The Kodak Theater was really nice. I'd watched American Idol season after season and would have never thought I would be in the audience watching one of my closest friends perform and it felt great. J.P. was able to get tickets for Lonnie to come to the show as well, and it was good seeing him again since I hadn't seen him since last year's fourth of July weekend. The trip to L.A. went by so fast we were only there for a total of three days and two nights. I had to get back and take my finals and Kenya's business was booming so she had to get back and oversee it. I ended the semester well and I decided to go back to the firm I was working at last year. I still hadn't decided whether or not I was going to take them up on their offer of permanent employment. I was currently looking for jobs in Atlanta while I still had time to make a final decision.

Now that Memorial Day weekend was here, I wanted Omar to stay at my apartment with me, but since his friends were in town and he was on the Board he was able to get a free suite at the host hotel. Since it was D.C.'s pride, I knew that we wouldn't be spending a lot of quality time together this weekend, as it would be filled with partying and clubbing all night. This was really starting to get old to me. I felt like the bulk of the time the two of us spent together revolved around going to a gay club. I liked to have a good time too, but some weekends I wanted to just go see a movie or sit in the house and rent a movie. I rarely got to see Omar since we didn't live in the same city. I hoped once we did move to the same area things would be a lot different because the club atmosphere had too much going on for two people who were trying to establish a relationship.

I picked Omar and his two friends up from the airport when they arrived on Friday night. I was so happy to see Omar and since I had so much going on the past month with finals and getting the year's final edition of the Georgetown Review out, I wasn't able to drive down and see him like I had been doing regularly. As soon as he had got in the car he gave me a big hug and a kiss and I had forgotten all about being indifferent about him partying all weekend long with his friends. We had talked about my concerns on the phone last night and he said one night he planned not to go out and we would do something special, just the two of us. I needed to hear that because I was really beginning to think that he was too consumed with the nightlife to ever be serious about me.

They were staying at the Renaissance, which was on 9th Street in northwest. When we got to the hotel there were plenty of people standing out front of the hotel loitering. By continuously attending these pride events, the loitering seemed to be something that was normal, and I always wondered what the hotel staff thought with all these black men just standing outside. David was hanging out with us this weekend. I was glad because he would be able to keep me from getting jealous while Omar worked the club and was in everyone's face promoting Atlanta pride, and his parties that he was going to have at the end of the summer.

David was in a bit of a depressed state and I had to convince him to come out with me tonight. Which was so not the norm between us; I was usually the one saying no and I was too busy. He had been dating a guy name Jay that hadn't been treating him as good as he should. David had this infatuation with boys who were near-straight, still dated women, had kids and sometimes were married. He mentioned to me that he met this guy online at a gay dating website on a Sunday. He said when he met Jay he was instantly attracted to him, they went back to David's house and watched TV and smoked a few blunts. Nothing sexual happened between the two of them the first night. The guy did ask David if he had any porn, and David was kind of taken off-guard and didn't have any tapes or DVDs. He assumed that he was trying to get them into a sexual mood. However, David was really feeling the guy and didn't want to move too fast so nothing happened between them that first night. The next couple of days they had hung out and smoked weed and David got to know Jay a little more. Come to find out, Jay was homeless and he sometimes escorted. That didn't stop David for falling for this guy and the following weekend they drove to Atlantic City and David won fifteen hundred dollars and gave Jay half because he thought it would help out since he was homeless and all. Of course he started coming around more, showing interest, and they went to Atlantic City the following weekend as well. David enjoyed his company and they were able to be alone, which David thought was romantic and gave him an opportunity to get to know Jay even more. However, the second time in Atlantic City David lost all his money plus money that he shouldn't have taken out of his savings account.

Since David was in a financial crunch when he returned from Atlantic City he wasn't able to buy weed or do the things that Jay wanted him to do. David was convinced that the guy liked him and would keep coming around. However, once the money stopped flowing the guy started acting different and was distant. David borrowed money from friends and relatives so that he could pay his bills, get to work and get Jay to come around again. But it wasn't enough and Jay stopped coming around, and by this time David had deep feelings.

I had met Jay one time when we had all went out to a pool party, and I could see why David liked him; he was very attractive. He looked like the rapper Nelly and the funny thing about it was he was from St. Louis, the same place Nelly was from.

David was depressed now because the guy was treating him terribly, telling David that he wasn't his type because he wasn't masculine enough. He said that he was only around because of the money and the only way he would have sex with him was in a threesome. This hurt David's self-esteem significantly. David started second guessing himself and started believing all the negative things that were being said. I kept telling him that the guy had serious issues and he needed to cut his losses and leave him alone. But no matter what I said David was too caught up in trying to make this guy change his mind. I really felt bad for David because he had a lot to offer anyone. He definitely had above-average looks; when we went out to clubs we both would get our fare share of digits. He needed to stop looking for love in all the wrong places I thought was the problem.

I knew he couldn't help who he fell in love with. But since he was so comfortable with his sexuality he needed to find someone who was equally comfortable, or find someone that accepted him for who he was. For some reason he thought he would be able to change these near-straight dudes into the man he wanted them to be. Maybe one day he would find someone that he could change, but I was almost certain that he would continue to get the same result messing with this sort of guy.

When David arrived at the hotel I could see the sadness in his eyes, and he didn't even mention all the fine boys standing outside the hotel. This was definitely not the same friend that I had grown to love. "Hey David, I am glad you could make it. Omar and his friends want to take a shower and get dressed so we can go out soon."

"Okay, that is fine. Hey everyone, it's good seeing you guys again!"

"Wassup David!" Everyone said in unison.

"Let's go downstairs and have a drink at the bar while they are getting ready," I suggested.

"That is fine with me," David replied as we walked out the hotel suite. "I actually need to vent anyway. Why did Jay call me tonight asking to borrow fifty dollars? I mean can I get a hello, how are you doing? All he does is ask me for stuff. I know he is looking for a job, but if he ain't fucking me or trying to be with me then he needs to stop calling me asking me for shit."

"Well boo, because you started off being so generous in the beginning and he is in need, and he knows you like him, and he thinks that shit is okay. You need to tell him that he needs to stop asking you."

"Trust me, I do, but all he does is get mad and says he never wants to talk or deal with me anymore."

"Well you know what I think, that is what you need to do; leave his broke ass alone."

"Easier said than done, I mean I know I need to but I want to be with this dude more than anything right now."

"Well do you know why you like him so much?"

"Dontae I have been asking myself this over and over again. I mean I know I am attracted to him and he is nice and charming most of the time. I just feel like if he treated me a lot better, we could really have something together."

"You still didn't tell me why you like him so much because the way it sounds he doesn't do anything that would warrant you to be going crazy over him."

"You're right he is such an asshole at times. I just can't explain why he is the only dude I want to be with. I wish I knew what made me so crazy about him. If I did then I would be able to make these feelings go away. I just want to go out tonight, enjoy myself, get really fucked up and hopefully meet someone to take my mind off Jay because if I don't I am going to lose my mind. There is no way I am going to break down over someone that says that I am not hot enough for them. I cannot believe he said that, he got me going to the gym every damn day trying to get my body together."

"David you are fine, please don't allow this guy to mess your head up, you are way too special to have to deal with something like this. You need to always remember that you have power, and you cannot relinquish your power to anyone because if you do then you lose yourself. I don't know what to do or say to get you back to your normal self, but I am going to try my best because I love you too much to see this happen to you."

"Thank you, I appreciate that, I just wish I knew where I went wrong, what happened with this guy. I have never in my life experienced this severity of rejection. I just wish I knew what was in his head so I could move on with my life. Our relationship is like a seesaw; there are times when I think I am getting in and then the next day he is telling me he never wants to see me again. I'm going to put this to bed for this weekend. I know you think I am crazy and you don't understand.

You have so much control over your life and you're not a mess like me. You get everything you want. You are in law school you have two guys that I would kill for, even deal with Darrel's bullshit if I had the chance. I go after the rejects because I think it would be easier to get them and make them fall in love with me, but they never do. I don't know what it is about me. Guys either want to have sex with me, and they don't want to have anything to do with me after they bust a nut, or they want to use me for whatever they think they can get. I cannot keep going through this, Dontae, I need to meet a good man to show me that I am worth what I think I am, that I am worthy of love."

"Trust me David, my life is not what you think it is, but I do think part of the problem is your self-esteem. Most people prey on the weak and if you allow someone to take advantage of you and they aren't good people then you lost control. Please understand the difference between someone liking you for you or liking you for what they can get from you. Maybe part of the problem is you are being superficial. You have to ask yourself: what does this guy have to offer me besides eye candy? Not to end this conversation so abruptly, but I think the more we talk about this the more you are not going to feel good about yourself, so lets just go have some fun. We need to be heading back upstairs anyway, they should be ready by now. I will pay for the drinks right now, but make sure you have your wallet out when we get to the club." I joked to brighten up the mood.

We both laughed and hugged each other, and I swore I saw a glimpse of tears coming down from my friends face. I acted like I didn't see it and went back upstairs to get the boys. I knew that he was still going to deal with Jay. I just hoped that Jay would realize what he had and started treating my friend better, or David moved on without getting his heart broken even further. Only time would tell. I knew David was a lot stronger than this, though, so I was hoping for the best. This moment of insanity was getting old and I knew he would look back at this situation and ask himself, "What have I done?"

EVEN THOUGH THIS WAS THE first night Omar was in town and I should have been focusing my attention in his direction, I really felt bad for David. I knew that Omar and I had plans to spend some one-on-one time this weekend so I dedicated tonight to making sure David and I had fun and that meant being tipsy, flirting and meeting the finest men who wanted to take us home. The only thing was I was hoping David got lucky and I didn't do anything to make Omar not trust me or think I wanted to be with anyone in the club besides him. He had never seen me in my element in D.C., where most of the people I had talked to and flirted with in the club assumed I was single and ready to mingle.

I knew a lot of people just from hanging out with David and going to the clubs. I really didn't know anyone on a personal level, just in a cordial how-you-doing way. I guess most thought that I was a mystery and wanted to get to know me. I didn't know what it was, but after I met someone they expected me to speak to them the next time I saw them. I kind of felt fake doing that because it wasn't like I really knew them, but I guess this was just part of the gay culture. David had mentioned to me that someone that he met or knew thought I was shady because I didn't speak to them when I saw them. I responded, "Probably because I don't know them." I thought it was silly when people thought I was shady, because most people who actually got to know me liked me a lot. I had just never and don't know if I would ever be the one who would initiate a friendship. It wasn't because I thought people should come up to me. I wasn't that conceited or into myself. It was more so that for whatever reason, I had always been hated on just for being me. And I had gotten so tired of asking for acceptance from people that I wanted to love me; to the point where I didn't even care who accepted me or not, which was why I shied away from people until I got some sort of positive vibe.

A part of me wanted to party with Omar and another part of me didn't want to. I didn't want any jealous drama on either part to occur. It was good to know that he was in the building. When my song came on or when David was hollering at a cutie I could meet up with Omar and we could do our thing on the dance floor. I loved when we got our freak on with each other while we were dancing. We would grind and kiss on the dance floor to a song and it was like foreplay, a prelude to what would be going down at the end of the night. This was something that I had been waiting weeks for, something that I couldn't wait to experience again. I guess this was what kept me coming back, and I hoped what kept him coming back was that we had great chemistry.

The night happened as planned and just before the club was about to close David and I hung out outside in his truck while Omar and his boys stayed inside until it closed. I was sitting in the front seat smoking a blunt, which I had been doing more and more lately, and enjoying the CD that David made with all the latest music on it. He was in the back seat talking to this guy we saw parked right next to us. When we exited the club the dude was standing out in front of his black Jaguar and was eyeing David as he walked to the driver's side of his truck. David noticed he was being watched and spoke to the guy, next thing I knew they were walking to the store to go get Black and Milds to smoke. I didn't smoke so much without being with David; he had me smoking weed and Black and Milds. I was sure my fellow classmates and professors wouldn't recognize me if they saw me.

When they got back from the store David and his new friend got in the back of the truck while I was inside. I couldn't really hear their conversation, because they were whispering, but I did notice they kept giggling. So I took this as my cue to stand outside the car and see what was going on in the parking lot. There were several guys outside cruising and making plans as to what they were going to do once the club let out. As I stood watching, people were hooking up from the club and walking to their cars to go home and get busy. This guy I had met at the Mill when I was hanging out with David came up to me to see what was up.

I never called him and that was the first thing he asked. "How come you never called?" I decided to tell him that I had a significant other and he wouldn't be too happy if I called you. He still tried to continue to flirt and miss the fact that I said that I had a boyfriend. In so many words he was like, "So what your boyfriend got to do with me?" The club was beginning to close and let out and the last thing I needed was for Omar to see this dude all up in my face. So I got rid of him real quick and as soon as I did there walks Omar and his buddies. He spotted me instantly and walked over to where I was standing. "Hey baby, did you enjoy yourself?" I said as he walked in earshot.

"Yeah baby, I did, but towards the end they were playing our song and you were nowhere to be found."

"My bad, David wanted to get some air, so I decided to step out. But we have plenty of time to hear our song."

"I know we do, and I see that David found the right time to go get some air. He got my baby standing outside while he is in the back doing God knows what," He kidded.

"Be quiet, David ain't like that, he just talking and this is good for him since he got his head so far stuck up this boy name Jay's ass."

"Aaight, well tell him we about to go, I am going to the car. Give me the keys." I handed over the keys, and he kissed me on my lips very passionately. So I knew I wouldn't be standing out here much longer. I needed to be with Omar tonight. So I told David that I would meet up with him tomorrow for round two and to text me when he made it to his destination to let me know he was okay.

NOW THAT SCHOOL HAD STARTED BACK and this was my last year I had finally decided that I would be moving to Atlanta and working for a large law firm. Unfortunately I was going to be practicing real estate law which I didn't really have much interest in, but the pay was terrific and this was the only job I could find that would put me closer to Omar. I knew if we wanted our relationship to work then I really needed to move. Going through the summer in D.C. with hardly anything to do after work but go out for drinks with David had almost gotten me into a lot of trouble. Everywhere I turned there was some dude wanting to hook up, and it was just my luck that most were dudes I really did want to hook up with. I had been so bored the entire summer. That I had gone out on dates with guys that I had met out. I was quick to inform them that I was not looking for anything serious. I was just trying to meet new people. Most of them had been real cool with that, but there was usually a lot of sexual tension that I had to endure during these encounters that drove me crazy.

I kept repeating to myself that long-distance relationships were not fun. I was excited I had this last year of school to keep me busy. Staying away from all these attractive men was becoming unbearable and I really didn't want to confuse things by getting with someone out of convenience. It was hard to resist temptation when you were lonely and in need of attention. My hand and my private parts had become best friends, and I had succumbed to late night phone sex with Omar to get me through our time apart. It was nothing like the real thing, but it beat jacking off by myself, plus I liked him letting me know what he was going to do with me the next time he saw me. It made me anticipate our next meeting even more.

School had become real mundane the last year. I was still loving it but I couldn't wait to finish. I wished the job that I was going to take would be something more up my alley but for some reason there were no offers on the table for entertainment or even criminal law. I had one other job offer in the Atlanta area with the federal government, but the pay wasn't enough and I had heard horror stories about federal employees and how the jobs were not rewarding. The only good thing I heard was that the benefits were really good as far as medical, dental and retirement. But the type of money I would be making in this firm would more than compensate for the good benefits that I would be passing up. The firm that I was working for had pretty good benefits anyway, so I would be good. I was hoping that I would work there for about three years and save enough money so that I could open up my own practice so I didn't have to work for anyone for the rest of my life and I could work at my own pace and schedule and enjoy life.

I really missed J.P. I knew she thought I had gotten her through the first year, but she equally got me through the first year. The second year I thought I was going to lose it without her. I just talked to her the other day; she called me from

Seattle where she was still on tour with American Idol. She would be here next month with the American Idol tour, and she had already given me my tickets. I was so proud of her; she was living her dream. She took a chance and it paid off. I doubted that she would ever go back to law school, but you never knew what life had in store for anyone. I just thought it was awesome that she was so talented and she had options. Although I missed our coffee runs, happy hours and late-night phone conversations, I knew we would be friends for life. Something about or green eyes connected us for eternity, and no mater what we would always stay in touch.

I was also glad that she introduced me to Kenya, who was also a wonderful person as well. Her business was a success. A lot of companies in the area were committed to helping her cause. In the summer I had the opportunity of introducing her to the recruiter who brought me into the firm where I worked over the summer. Once I had told the recruiter about Kenya's devotion to make sure the natives of D.C. were able to find employment, they readily signed up and now used her agency when looking for temporary or temp-to-perm employees. She even had plans on opening offices in New York City and Atlanta in a few years. Kenya was amazing and had vision. There were not too many people that I knew like her. Shit, I didn't even know if I could have pulled something like that off.

Kenya and I had dinner and she told me about an incident that she had with a football player that she was engaged to by the name of Cordel. She said that after she stopped seeing him she was in such a wreck that all she could do to remain sane was to work and dream about a better life. She had grown up poor and never wanted to go without a day in her life. She told Cordel all about her past and he promised to take care of her, he had told her she wouldn't want for anything. She knew he had a drug problem, she never brought it to anyone's attention and never brought it up to him that she even knew. She had been around drugs all her life, so she knew the signs, but everything was working out with them and their relationship, so she thought she could deal with it until the unthinkable happened.

She said that Cordel had gotten back in touch with her because he saw an article about her business in Jet magazine and he called the office. She didn't return any of his calls at first but one Friday when she was working late he showed up at the office and she was the only one working. Her receptionist had forgotten to lock the door. She said she was shocked when she first saw him and wanted to call security immediately, but there was something in his eyes that let her know that she should listen to him. Kenya packed up her things and they went to dinner. Cordel confessed that he was still in love with her and that he would do anything to get her back. He told her that he didn't expect her to make up her mind today but he would be wearing her down in the meantime. Kenya confessed to me that she had never fell out of love with Cordel and that she did love him, but she didn't know how to forgive him for what he had done to Jennifer. She said all she could think about was what he did every time she thought about him, and started seeing a therapist to help her get over her pain and learn to forgive. I was kind of shocked to hear this coming from her because Kenya always seemed a step ahead of everyone. I knew from hanging out with her that she rarely dated anyone seriously and didn't have any real prospects that she ever mentioned.

I personally felt she should give this guy another chance, especially if she still had feelings for him. Drugs could mess up a lot, including a relationship. I knew this firsthand from having dealt with my mother. The hardest thing to do was forgive someone who had really hurt you, but to love the person who had hurt you I didn't know how she was going to do this. I prayed that she did because she deserved to be happy and it sounded like this guy really was sorry and had gotten his life back on track. I thought to myself after having this conversation that you never really knew what a person was going through. You could look at someone and they seemed like they had it all together, because they drove a nice car, lived in a big house, and had a great job but we all had our issues, including me.

The issues are what makes life so hard and being able to deal with them successfully allows for a much more sane life. I have seen so many people turn to drugs, alcohol and sex to help them cope with their issues, not realizing that all they have to do is take time out to process and analyze what is going on. Moments of reflection and talking through situations are the best mechanisms to cope. Not understanding what is truly going on with yourself or what is making you unhappy will eat at you until you don't recognize yourself and people don't even recognize who you are anymore. I personally don't believe that anyone can make decisions for anyone else. That is why God gave each and every one of us a brain, and the will to do what we want. Always having control of your emotions and actions leads to a more peaceful existence. Of course we all have our moments when we don't see clearly and we let someone else dictate what we should or shouldn't do. But this should be rare and not something someone one should do for long periods of time or rely on. If someone is offering you good insight or advice to lead you in the right direction of course listen to them, but how you flip it and apply it to your life makes the difference. There is no way anybody can mimic or do exactly what someone else does and get the same results in life. It is good to have role models, but it is the positive attributes one takes from those role models that is going to sustain that individual.

I know I don't know everything and I know I have made mistakes and will continue to make mistakes, but I am very proud that I am of sound body and spirit. That I have control over my desires, wants and dislikes and I will be damned if I am going to let anyone take that control away from me. If I did then I wouldn't be Dontae Erickson and I have come a long way from that timid little boy in search of love and acceptance from people who don't have my best interest in mind and probably never will.

EPILOGUE

Jennifer Peale

I must admit moving to D.C. was absolutely positively the best decision I could have made. Who would have thought that I would be in the studio right now working on my very own album? The American Idol tour was everything that I could have imagined it would be and as soon as I finished there were several labels begging me to sign with them including daddy's. In the end I wound up signing with my father because I knew he would take good care of me and when I was doing my interviews a lot of the record executives I really didn't trust. As soon as the tour ended Kurt and I got married in Vegas. After I finish my album we plan to have a huge wedding party for all our friends and family. He truly is a godsend and I can't imagine my life without being his wife.

Kenya and Cordel have started seeing each other again, which I am happy to report. She deserves someone special and I really think Cordel is the one for her. Veronica is expecting twins in a couple of months so I will have two baby brothers shortly which I am very excited about. I still cannot believe daddy at his age is going to be a father of newborns, but hey they are happy and that is all I could ask for.

Monica was the first person to get booted from the finals, but at least she made it and we were able to go on tour together. Daddy offered her a record deal as well, but she decided that she would go with another label that was more focused on the kind of music that she wanted to put out. I couldn't blame her for that and I hoped we kept in touch. My life has been such an amusement park ride that has still not finished yet. I am looking forward to the future and hoping that this dream doesn't end anytime soon.

Dontae Erickson

I am sitting in my office looking over Peachtree Street in Atlanta and I am overcome with joy that I have the letters Esq. at the end of my name. Although Clair Huxtable is the reason I went to law school, I am more than certain that my life will not mirror hers, for millions of reasons. Omar and I bought a home together in Stone Mountain in a new development with three levels, five bedrooms and three baths. This is my dream home and coming home to Omar everyday has been a dream come true. It has been all that and much more. I am still convincing him to get out of the party promotion business, to no avail, but I have learned to get over my jealous habits and focus on the fact that if he wanted to be with those "chicken heads" in the club he wouldn't be sleeping next to me every night.

David finally graduated and moved on from Jay. He is still single, partying and living it up in D.C. He says that he wants to move out here with me and I told him that he should but he hasn't yet. Although I am with Omar, I really don't like living in Atlanta. D.C. had a lot more to do and this place seems really slow for me. However, work is long and I usually don't get home until after nine at night. I was told that it is like this for the first year, so I have been sucking it up, but I swear I am in a modern day corporate sweatshop. I guess you got to work hard for this kind of money and nothing in life is ever free, even when you think it is.

CPSIA information can be obtained
at www.ICGtesting.com
Printed in the USA
BVOW08s0921200517
484582BV00001B/5/P

9 781607 430278